I Need a Hero

Also by Codi Gary

The Rock Canyon, Idaho Series
Bad For Me
Return of the Bad Girl
Bad Girls Don't Marry Marines
Good Girls Don't Date Rock Stars
Things Good Girls Don't Do
The Trouble with Sexy (a novella)

I Need a Hero

A MEN IN UNIFORM NOVELLA

CODI GARY

AVONIMPULSE
An Imprint of HarperCollinsPublishers

This is a work of fiction. Names, characters, places, and incidents are products of the author's imagination or are used fictitiously and are not to be construed as real. Any resemblance to actual events, locales, organizations, or persons, living or dead, is entirely coincidental.

Excerpt from *One Lucky Hero* copyright © 2016 by Codi Gary.
Excerpt from *The Bride Wore Red Boots* copyright © 2015 by Lizbeth Selvig.
Excerpt from *Rescued by the Ranger* copyright © 2015 by Dixie Lee Brown.
Excerpt from *One Scandalous Kiss* copyright © 2015 by Christy Carlyle.
Excerpt from *Dirty Talk* copyright © 2015 by Megan Erickson.

EPub Edition OCTOBER 2015 ISBN: 9780062441249

Print Edition ISBN: 9780062441256

AM 10 9 8 7 6 5 4 3 2 1

Chapter One

OLIVER MARTINEZ SAT stiffly in the wobbly office chair, the room stifling despite the hum of the air conditioner above his head. He wasn't usually the nervous type, being that military police didn't allow time for panic, but facing off against General Reynolds, the man who pretty much held his career in the palm of his hand...

Well, he figured he had a right to sweat with the way the older man was staring him down.

"What do you have to say for yourself, Sergeant?" General Reynolds asked.

A thousand excuses ran through his mind, but none of them would appease the general, Oliver knew that. He hadn't become an MP to be liked; even his family knew he wasn't a people person. He was hardworking, sharp as a tack, and a mean son of a bitch when you got on his bad side—qualities that made him an excellent MP. And military police was exactly where Oliver belonged. He got to bust heads and keep order; it was structured, and there were rules. He was the good guy.

But this time, he had stepped in a big old pile of shit trying to play the hero.

"I did what I thought was right, sir," Oliver said.

"You instigated a confrontation with a civilian that turned into an all-out bar brawl," General Reynolds said. Although his tone and outward expression seemed calm, Oliver hadn't missed the eye twitch on the left side of the general's face. The man was beyond furious, and nothing Oliver did or said was going to make things better for him.

Why had he decided to go out with the guys on Friday? His buddies from group therapy, Dean Sparks and Tyler Best, had convinced him that he needed to get out and blow off some steam. He hadn't expected to take down some rowdy kid or have the cops called on them. The civilian police had been cool, though, once he explained the situation, and as they hauled the kid off for drunk and disorderly, he'd thought that was the end of it.

Until he'd shown up for work this morning only to have Tate tell him he wasn't on rotation and that the general wanted to see him. Oliver hadn't had any idea what the meeting was about, but he'd never expected to get his ass chewed over something that wasn't even his fault.

"It wasn't a brawl, sir. I contained and subdued him too fast for that."

Oliver regretted his words the moment they left his mouth. They sounded arrogant, and that wasn't going to score him any points.

Especially since the civilian in question was the general's son.

Despite knowing this, Oliver tried again to explain his side. "I just mean, and with all due respect, sir, that the civilian was drunk and harassing several women, and when I politely asked him to leave them alone, he threw the first punch."

General Reynolds's salt and pepper mustache twitched, and Oliver wondered for half a second if the general was messing with him and if he was secretly amused that his son had been taught a lesson in respect.

"I don't care if he threw a hundred punches. You should not have engaged. You did not have to break his nose or sprain his wrist while you were restraining him."

Okay, so he wasn't amused. But no matter how angry the general might be, Oliver wasn't going to apologize for roughing up the little punk. The kid had thrown a sucker punch that had lit fire to Oliver's jaw, and it was still sore. And if the kid hadn't fought him so damn hard, he wouldn't have gotten hurt in the first place.

Would he have handled things differently if he'd known who the kid's dad was? Maybe. But there was nothing Oliver could do about it now except take whatever punishment was meted out to him.

"It seems to me you could use a little time out of the field to learn how to channel your aggression...in other ways," General Reynolds said.

Now the general was smiling, and unease swept over Oliver.

"Have you heard of the Alpha Dog Training Program?" General Reynolds asked.

"Yeah, I know a few of the guys running things," Oliver said.

And neither Best nor Sparks had been happy about it at first. The Alpha Dog Training Program was the brainchild of some PR expert hoping to create a good public image for the military by training shelter dogs for specialty jobs like military, fire, police, search and rescue, and therapy. And if the animals-getting-a-second-chance angle didn't just make you weepy, the dogs were being trained by troubled kids under the supervision of MPs.

It was meant as an alternative punishment for nonviolent juvenile offenders. Instead of being locked up in a detention center with months of community service tacked on top, they were sent to Alpha Dog. They shoveled shit, fed and cared for the dogs, and learned how to teach them basic obedience. The place was set up with barracks for up to twenty-five kids at a time. The goal was to give them a skill and refocus their energies. The program even helped them with job placement at several Sacramento veterinary hospitals and rescue organizations. It was a better deal than most kids in the system got.

"Well, I'm glad you're familiar with it, because you're going to help organize and promote their upcoming charity event," General Reynolds said.

Oliver choked in surprise. "I don't know anything about fundraising!"

The general's eyes narrowed and glittered. "Well, this will give you a chance to develop a new skill."

Oliver just sat there, weighing his options. If he pitched a fit and accused the general of abusing his power because Oliver had hurt his son's delicate feelings, he'd be committing career suicide.

"How long will I be out of the field, sir?" he asked.

"Until I think you're ready," General Reynolds said.

Oliver nodded grimly. The only option open to him was to bite the bullet and do the job.

"You'll report to the Alpha Dog Training Program today. The event coordinator will be there at eleven to give you instructions on what you'll be doing. I do hope you take this time to learn some discipline, Sergeant Martinez."

Fuck you.

Taking a deep breath, Oliver stood up and saluted the general. As soon as he barked, "Dismissed," Oliver was out the door, wishing he was headed home to beat the hell out of his punching bag. This whole morning had sucked donkey nuts, and the last thing Oliver wanted to do was be around a bunch of teenagers or his friends.

Not that Best and Sparks weren't good people, but he knew that the minute they found out about his little time-out, they were going to laugh it up.

Especially Best.

OLIVER PARKED HIS car and wondered how in the hell a building that held dozens of dogs was so quiet.

Not that there would be anyone around to be bothered by the noise; Alpha Dog Training Center sat on several acres. The closest neighbors were a couple of farms. The facility was a two-story, solid brick building surrounded by a landscape of cactuses and desert plants.

Probably trying to save water during the drought.

The cement walkway led to glass double doors through which Oliver saw Best before he even stepped inside. In the twenty minutes it had taken him to get to his car and drive off base to the Alpha Dog Training Center in North Sac, he had tried prepare himself for his friends' reactions to his news.

He stepped inside. "What's up, Best?"

Oliver's voice echoed in the large, open front of the facility, and Best swung his way, his eyes widening. "Martinez? What are you doing in this neck of the woods?"

Oliver crossed the linoleum floor and slapped Best on the back. "Let's just say that I got reassigned."

"What, here? Well, hell, man, I could use you. Why didn't you tell us? You know, if you haven't taken the training course for handling military dogs, I can make a phone call."

"I just found out I was assigned here. Where's Sparks at?" Oliver definitely didn't want to tell this story twice.

"He's in the back talking to one of the kids' parents. She came in hot about something, and I showed her to the 'director's' office." Best snorted, as if Sparks wasn't cut out for running this operation. But Oliver had known Sparks longer. He was more than equipped to handle an irate parent. The guy was on his way to general someday if he could just get his psychiatrist to give him a pass. Sparks suffered from PTSD and survivor's guilt after his last tour. Despite months spent in individual and group therapy, his shrink kept telling him he still needed time before she'd clear him. It pissed him off royally, but he'd seemed to become less restless since being assigned to Alpha Dog.

Oliver followed Best down the hall until a door on the end swung open and a robust black woman stepped out, smiling. "Thank you for taking the time to talk to me about your program, Sergeant Sparks. When they told me my Keenan had been transferred here, I didn't know what to think."

Sparks stepped out after her, and although he wasn't smiling, his tone was reassuring. "I assure you, Mrs. Washington, he is in good hands, and hopefully we can help get him back on track."

The woman actually simpered at Sparks, and Oliver shook his head. Sparks's normal countenance was somber—he was a bigger hard-ass than Oliver by a long shot—yet he never seemed to have trouble charming women. Even when Oliver's married sister, Luz, had visited and met Sparks, she had fawned all over him. When Oliver had given her hell about it, she'd said she could never resist a brooding hero.

And yet, her overly friendly, computer geek husband belied her words.

"Martinez, why are you looking at me as if you want to kiss me?" Sparks asked.

Oliver realized that the woman had left while he was spaced out and shoved Sparks. "Kiss you? Who would want to kiss your ugly mug?"

Sparks's dark eyes narrowed. "Ugly my ass; I'm as pretty as a fucking daisy."

"Shit, I'm a daisy; you're more like one of those this-tles that grow where no one wants them," Best said.

"A limp daisy," Sparks fired back.

The bickering was actually making Oliver feel a little better about being there. He could handle a few weeks at this place if it meant being around his boys. As for the charity event, he'd follow the publicist's rules and coast through it, just like he had with high school math. How hard could it be?

"HOLY SHIT, YOU got screwed!" Best howled with laughter.

"Glad the injustice of my situation gives you the jol-lies, dick," Oliver said. The three of them had filed into Sparks's office, and Oliver had given them the lowdown.

And just as he'd suspected, they were models of empathy.

Best continued to hoot, his tall frame bent over, and his shaved blond head the only thing Oliver could see.

Sparks at least had the decency to cover his laugh with a cough. Where Best had the California surfer look, Sparks had eyes as dark as flint and a thick, muscular body to Best's leaner one.

Sparks recovered first. "So, when is your new keeper supposed to be here?"

Oliver looked up at the clock. "Eleven, so I've got about fifteen minutes to kill. You mentioned you could use me, Best. For what?"

"I need another military dog trainer today," Best said. "Sparks is going to work with the search-and-rescue dogs, and he's got about five kids he's training. I have my hands full with eight of my own."

"I'm not sure how much help I'll be able to give. It all depends on what this publicist has for me. The last thing I need is for them to report back that I'm not pulling my weight."

"I wouldn't worry about it, man. They're going to realize that they picked the wrong guy for this gig, and they'll probably do most of the work themselves, anyway," Sparks said.

"And how much do you really think goes into a charity event? Couple of phone calls and boom, you'll be done, bored, and looking for something to do," Best said.

Before Oliver could answer, a knock sounded on Sparks's office door. Best reached out and opened it, his eyes widening a bit.

And then, the sexiest woman Oliver had ever seen glided in, smiling as her gaze landed on each of them in turn.

Then those green eyes met his, and he forgot how to breathe.

"Hello, I'm Evelyn Reynolds, the publicist hired to organize Alpha Dog's upcoming charity event." She held her hand out to him, and Oliver took it, the soft press of her palm warm against his. Oliver's skin suddenly prickled with heat all the way up his arm. "I am so happy to be handling this project. If there is one thing that the world loves, it's saving animals."

Oliver nodded, barely listening. He hadn't exactly known what to expect of his new boss, but it definitely wasn't a woman who looked like a '50s pinup model in a polka-dot pencil skirt and black framed glasses. His *abuela* loved old movies, and he'd watched them with her enough to know what he liked: curvy women with class.

And damn if this woman didn't fit the bill.

Her dark hair was swept back in some kind of updo—the fact that he even knew that just proved how much having two little sisters had warped his brain. She wore a short sweater over a red top that hugged a set of breasts that would have made a saint stare.

Oliver grinned. He'd never been in the running for sainthood anyway.

"Are you okay?" she asked.

"Hmm?"

"I was just wondering if you were going to let me have my hand back." Her tone was brimming with amusement, and one of her dark brows was arched.

Oliver lost his smile and heard Best laugh again. Releasing her, he ran his hand over the back of his neck, knowing he was probably blushing like an idiot.

"Sorry, ma'am," he muttered.

"I'm Sergeant Sparks, program director." Sparks had come around the desk, drawing the attention away from Oliver for a second, giving him a chance to get a grip. She was just a woman. Sure, an extremely hot woman, but that didn't mean he needed to act like an idiot.

"It's good to meet you," Evelyn said to Sparks.

"And I'm Sergeant Best." Best had come up alongside her, and when he took her hand, Oliver saw the wink he gave her. "But you can call me Tyler."

Oliver caught a growl in his throat. Best flirted with all women, Oliver knew that, but watching him do it with Evelyn twisted his guts up, and it was ridiculous. He had just met her and hadn't exactly given a great first impression.

"And you can call me Ms. Reynolds, Sergeant Best."

Oliver scoffed, happy that she hadn't fallen for Best's act. And then something struck him.

Reynolds? As in General Reynolds?

"And the slow one is Sergeant Martinez," Best said helpfully.

If she hadn't turned back to look at him, Oliver would have flipped Best off. *I'm going to kick his ass.*

Those big, beautiful eyes watched him with curiosity and something else he couldn't place. If the general was her father, had he told her who Oliver was?

"Sergeant Martinez, I believe you're helping me out on this project," she said.

Well, she doesn't sound vindictive. But she did sound a little disappointed. Why, though?

"Yes, ma'am," he said.

"Is there a place we can set up?" she asked.

"There is a conference room down the hall and to the right of the lobby," Sparks said.

Hiking her shoulder bag higher, she said, "Shall we get started, Sergeant?"

Chapter Two

EVELYN REYNOLDS HAD been around military men all her life, and there was a very good reason why she didn't get involved with them.

Actually, there were a buttload of reasons, but they all boiled down to her father. He had always been adamant about her not getting involved with a military man, but even if he had been okay with it, she'd have steered clear. She'd spent her childhood watching her mother worry and fret when her dad was gone, and she did not want that life.

However, that didn't mean she couldn't look and admire the hot piece of man in uniform standing in front of her. He was taller than her five feet four inches by almost a foot, with tan skin and eyes that looked like the ocean off of the Honolulu beach she'd loved to swim in when her father had been stationed there. This man's shoulders were wide and tapered down into a V at his waist. His pants were slightly baggy, but she had a feeling he had an ass you could bounce a quarter off of.

If Evelyn had a weakness, it was a man with a great ass.

But it was her reaction to Sergeant Martinez that was making her uneasy. The man had said a total of four words to her, but his deep timbre had made her tingle all over, something that had never happened.

"How about we head out to this little café I know?" he said. "I'm starving."

They had just left Sergeant Sparks's office, and his suggestion surprised her. She'd thought maybe he was just taciturn, one of those strong silent types, but maybe he had been as thrown by her as she was by him.

The idea delighted her more than she liked.

"I already ate, thanks." Actually, all she'd had was a protein bar and a bottle of water because she'd been too busy to stop and eat, but there was no way she was going to brunch or lunch or whatever with this man. It might give him the wrong impression.

"All due respect, but I can be a bit of a bear when I don't eat. How about we eat and in return, I'll do whatever you need me to for this shindig," Oliver said.

His suggestion rankled Eve; it was the same kind of thing her father did, trying to manage her life. Like when he'd told her that he'd only pay for colleges within a ten-hour car ride. Or when she'd come back from her first semester with pink tips and he'd commanded that she stop dyeing her hair "strange" colors. The trouble with commanding her, which her dad still hadn't learned, was that she was too much like him to bend over and take orders from any man. Which is why she'd gotten a scholarship to Hart University in Hart, Mississippi—four days of driving away—but there was little he could do once she'd accepted. And even less when she'd come back the next summer with fire-engine red hair.

When she'd graduated with her business degree, she'd lived in LA for a while, interning at a large PR firm, but when they'd offered her a position, she'd turned it down. It was an incredible opportunity, but she'd hated LA. So, she'd moved home and made a website, launching her own publicity management company, Reynolds Relations. Granted, it was a one-woman operation, but she was just getting started.

Eve knew she was lucky that her dad had called her about the Alpha Dog Training Program. If she could put together an amazing event for the US military, it would put her name on the map.

But fraternizing with Sergeant Martinez was not part of the plan, and that's what would happen if they went to eat. They'd talk about things other than the project and she'd fall behind, all because she couldn't say no to those beautiful blue eyes.

"As hungry as you might be, I think you can wait until our meeting is over to go grab something," she said.

"Actually, I'm hypoglycemic. I have to eat every few hours or I could die."

"Really? It's amazing you've lasted in the armed forces so long. You know, since they're usually not so accommodating to specific eating schedules."

"What can I say? I'm special," he said.

Eve bit back a smile. "I'm sure you are."

"Now, I know you don't mean that as a compliment, but I'm going to take it as one," he said. "Come on, you can't eat and work at the same time?"

No, bad idea. Get things back on track.

"Sergeant Martinez, I don't want to stand here arguing about this. If you so desperately need to eat, then fine, we'll go elsewhere to work. But we *will* be working."

"Yes, ma'am," he said.

Eve sighed and walked toward the exit, the heavy sound of his boots following behind her. She was weak. That was the only explanation for how easily she'd given into him. But she would keep the focus on the event and nothing else. No personal questions. She could handle sharing a meal with the man.

It wasn't that Sergeant Martinez made her uncomfortable—far from it. It was her reaction to him, from the moment their eyes had met, that threw her for a loop. The last thing she needed was to get involved with a military man, a lifer like her dad who put his country before everything else, even his family.

She wanted a life with a man who would be home every night. A life in which they'd make dinner together. Those hopes were why she also avoided ER doctors, pilots, lawyers…Basically any job with long hours and business trips were crossed off the potential husband list. She just wanted a normal, decent guy with a nine-to-five job who would love every crazy hair on her head.

Sure, she hadn't found that guy yet, but she was only twenty-five, after all. She had time. All she knew was that she wasn't going to find the man of her dreams in the military.

They walked through the doors, and a sheen of sweat instantly formed on Eve's skin as the hot summer air hit her. She was overdressed for June, but the sweater covered up the red halter top, making it more business casual. Once she took it off, she'd be ready to go out for drinks with her best friends tonight.

"I'm parked right there," he said.

"And I'm parked over here." She stopped next to her red Mini Cooper with a smirk. "I'll follow you."

"There's no sense in us taking two cars, and besides, we can work on the way."

"Sorry, cowboy, but I don't get in the cars of strange men," she said.

Eve could almost hear the gears in Sergeant Martinez's head turning, and finally, he shoved his keys back into his pocket. "Fine, I'll ride with you."

"Yeah, you probably don't want to do that," she said.

Sergeant Martinez had already rounded to the passenger side of her car. "What, are you a bad driver?"

"*Scary driver* is the term polite people use," she said.

"Well, if you're going to kill me, you might as well call me Oliver."

EVE DROVE TOWARD the café, weaving through the cars like a speed racer and grinning with every grunt from the man next to her. She could tell he was dying to say something about her driving, but instead, he kept his mouth shut and never once told her to slow down.

She liked that. Some guys could be such whiners.

But she still wasn't sure why she'd agreed to this. It wasn't just that he was pretty to look at; she'd been attracted to a number of men over the years but had never even been tempted to break her number one rule: no fraternizing with unsuitable men. It was a big deal to her, and yet, here she was, ignoring the little voice screaming at her to turn the car around and go back to the program building.

No, she was pretty sure it was that he'd surprised her. Oliver had completely thrown her off her game and broken down her defenses. She'd thought he was shy and awkward when they met in the office, especially with the way the other men had teased him, but the minute they'd been alone, he'd become charming and funny.

Damn it, why did he have to be funny?

"So, your last name is Reynolds, huh? As in General Reynolds?"

Eve had been waiting for him to make the connection between her and her dad and was surprised it had taken him so long. "Yep, he's my dad."

"So, did he actually hire you for this or strong-arm you into helping out?"

It was a valid question that anyone who knew her dad would ask, but she still stiffened, ready to defend him. It was one thing for her to think he was an overbearing ass sometimes, but she didn't like other people alluding to it.

"He hired me to help me out. I just started my PR company a few months ago, and this event could be great for my career," she said. "How did you draw the short straw of helping me out?"

"Well, I didn't volunteer," he said.

"I didn't think so." She swerved into the left lane and hit the gas to pass a minivan going ten miles under the speed limit. "Asshole."

"I'm assuming you aren't talking to me?" he asked.

"People should not get on the freeway if they don't know how to drive," she said.

"Agreed."

"Sorry, I have a bit of a road rage issue. It's one of my many flaws." *So much for not getting personal.* "Anyways, not many guys want to plan parties. At least, not many straight ones."

"Is that your way of asking me if I'm on the down low?" he asked.

Eve's cheeks burned because that was exactly what she'd been doing. "No, of course not. It's none of my business what team you bat for."

He laughed, the deep rumble sending a quiver through her body. "Since we're talking about it, I like women."

What kind of women, I wonder.

She didn't ask, though, because that was definitely something personal, and she'd already overstepped the line with him. Several times.

"I also happen to have two younger sisters. Twins. And after helping with *quinceañeras*, proms, and weddings, I will probably be more help than you think."

The information was delivered with a touch of exasperation, but beneath it was a warm tone she recognized.

An affection that said he loved his family no matter how much they aggravated him and would lay down his life for them.

Eve knew that tone well. It was the same one she used when talking about her brother and parents. Even when they were making her nuts, family was family.

"*Quinceañeras?*" She'd heard the word and knew it was some kind of party, but that was about it.

"Yeah, when a girl turns fifteen, her parents throw a huge party to celebrate," he said. "Fancy dresses, lots of people. It's a big deal. You want to get off on Tenth and make a left."

"Wow. All I got for my fifteenth birthday was my permit and gift cards." She exited the freeway and turned left.

"Yeah, I can't remember my fifteenth birthday. It's more of a girl thing. Besides, I'm not sure I'd look good in a ball gown," he said. "It's up there on the left."

Liar. You'd probably look good in anything.

"So, what's your plan for this thing, anyway?" he asked.

Gripping the steering wheel, she made a sharp left into the café parking lot, the sound of a horn blaring loudly as she crossed in front of several cars. "I was thinking a bachelor auction."

As she parked, Oliver scoffed. "I don't think you'll get very many volunteers for something like that."

"I wasn't talking about you guys. I was talking about the dogs," she said. She climbed out of the car and smoothed her skirt. She liked to at least look put together, even if it wasn't how she felt.

"The dogs? Seriously? How is that going to work?" Oliver caught up with her just as she stepped onto the sidewalk in front of the café and reached past her to get the door. Before she could walk through, three women in their early forties came out, eyeing Oliver like he was a piece of smooth milk chocolate.

"Ladies, have a good day," Oliver said behind her. He had moved closer, pressing his big, muscular body against her back, and she felt drops of perspiration run down her forehead that had nothing to do with the heat. No, her sudden rise in temperature definitely had more to do with Oliver's proximity.

"You, too," one of the ladies said, while the other two giggled.

When they were far enough away, Eve asked, "You got a thing for cougars?"

"Cougars? Come on, they weren't old enough to be my mother," he said.

Eve stepped into the café with a snort. "I see you didn't answer my question."

"This way." Oliver pointed, indicating a table free in the middle. Once they were seated, he added, "Are you asking because you really want to know?"

"Honestly, it's none of my business the kind of women you like." Eve grabbed a paper menu from the holder behind the salt and pepper, cursing silently. She couldn't seem to curb her reaction to him. Yes, she wanted to know what kind of women he liked, but she had no right to ask. She would just be setting him up to think she was interested in whatever he had, but she didn't want complicated and she definitely didn't need heartache. "I was just making an observation."

"But you're curious," Oliver prodded.

Eve looked up and met the blue depths of his eyes, but she was unprepared for the heat in them. Or the challenge. Whatever answer he had waiting for her was a loaded one, and she knew she shouldn't ask.

"Are you ready to order?" the server asked, coming up alongside their table. She was a young African American woman with brightly colored string weaved into her intricate braids, and she looked weary.

"Actually, I need a few minutes," Eve said, glancing at Oliver.

"I'll just have a coke for now," he said.

"Okay, I'll come back in a few minutes," the server said.

But before she could leave, Eve said, "I have to tell you, I love your hair."

The server's face brightened. "Thank you, I just got it done a few days ago."

"Well, it's fabulous, and I love the colors," Eve said.

"Thank you." As she walked away, Eve noticed a new skip in the woman's step and couldn't stop grinning as she looked at her menu.

"That was nice of you," Oliver said.

Eve glanced up at him and raised her eyebrow. "What? Telling her I like her hair? I do."

"I think it was more about making her feel good, though. Am I right?" Oliver said.

Eve shrugged. "She looked like she was having a bad day."

Oliver laughed, and she glared at him suspiciously. "What?"

"Nothing, it's just... You're so nice," he said.

"And?"

"I'm just thinking you must have gotten it from your mother," Oliver said.

Bristling, she slapped her menu down. "You don't know my dad. You know the general, your boss."

Oliver's dark eyebrows rose, and his eyes danced with amusement. "Well, *that's* something you got from *him*."

"My ability to call it like I see it?"

"Actually, I was going to say your protectiveness of your family, which is just like him," Oliver said.

For a moment, his answer stunned her, and she could feel the warmth of embarrassment staining her cheeks.

"Thank you," she said quietly.

"You're welcome."

Chapter Three

OLIVER COULD TELL he'd unsettled Eve, but the server's return crushed whatever moment they'd been having. After asking if they were serving lunch yet, Eve ordered a burger and fries with a Coke. Oliver wondered what her story was. She wasn't wearing a wedding ring, but that didn't mean anything these days.

"And how about you?" the server asked.

"Hot roast beef sandwich with extra barbeque sauce and fries," he said.

"All right, I'll get these put in and have them out as soon as they're ready."

As she walked away, Oliver opened his mouth to ask Eve about herself, but she cut him off.

"Okay, I think we should just stick to planning the event and spend less time talking about our personalities." Eve pulled out several color-coded folders with a rainbow of sticky notes poking out from the top and a planner so worn and thick it was held together by hot pink and black duct tape decorated with little white skulls.

Oliver fought another grin. *How in the hell did the general raise someone like you?*

As she flipped the folder open, she started in, talking fast. "So, I think we should have a family-friendly environment. Have the dogs' temperaments been tested?"

"Um, I'm not sure. Sergeant Best would be a better choice for that question, since this is only my first day," Oliver said.

"You don't know anything about the program?" she asked.

"Not much. Best and Sparks are friends of mine, so I know a little, but—"

"Why would they assign you to help out with PR if you know nothing about the program?"

"Well, actually, your father just assigned me this morning. He said it was an opportunity for me to learn discipline," he said.

"What did you do to deserve that?" she asked.

"Got your brother arrested," he said. It had come out blunter than he'd meant it to, but he wasn't going to lie about it. True, this might blow any chance he had with her, but—

Whoa, chance? She is the general's daughter, dude. You shouldn't even been thinking about chances.

"Well, that would definitely do it. How did you get him arrested?"

"He was wasted and hitting on some women who weren't interested. When I suggested he leave them alone, he took a swing at me and I put him down. Cops were called—"

"And as soon as you mentioned you were military, they let you off the hook," she said.

Her tone was snide, and anger coursed through him. "Actually, the fact that I was sober and your brother was mouthing off made my side of things pretty cut and dry. And for the record, I'm not sure what kind of pull my military status would have with civilian cops."

After a moment of silence, she said, "I'm sorry."

Oliver's temper cooled slightly at her apology, but knowing she was off limits made his reaction to her harder to take. Every time she blinked those thick black lashes or pursed her bee-stung lips, his cock twitched in frustration, and it was crazy. He shouldn't care what she thought about him. This was temporary. This was just one side-step in his career, and soon he'd be back to doing what he did best. It didn't matter how attracted he was to her. If landing the general's son in jail had gotten him here, he couldn't imagine what nailing the general's daughter would get him. Maybe a few weeks in the brig?

Or he'll just kill me and make sure my body is never found.

Regardless of the consequences, Oliver could not go there with her. He just needed to get over it. To think about something else.

"Don't worry about it," he said.

Awkward silence descended on them, but luckily their food arrived. Oliver picked up the top bun of his sandwich and dumped the extra barbeque sauce over the meat.

"So, what exactly do you need me to do for this thing?" he asked.

"Well, once I find out more about the dogs, I can start making a list of venues to contact."

He looked up from what he was doing in time to watch her take a huge bite of her burger and chew it slowly with her eyes closed for half a second. After she swallowed, she released a little sigh and licked her lips.

"Man, I love a good burger, don't you?" she asked.

Oliver nodded, even as his dick hardened. When had a woman eating become so fucking arousing? Or maybe it was just the look of pure bliss on her face that was turning him on?

And, damn, but he liked how secure she was in her own skin. Some girls would order a salad or cut their burger in half and chew tiny little bites behind their hands, but not Eve. She dived in and ate with gusto.

"Do I have mustard on my face?" She picked up her napkin and dabbed at her mouth. "Sorry, but I have been living on protein bars for days and it is awesome to sit down and eat."

"I thought you weren't hungry," he said, grinning.

She looked sheepish. "That was when I was trying to be professional."

"Since when is sharing a meal unprofessional?" he asked.

Oliver noticed the red stain of her cheeks and wondered what she was thinking.

"It can be too casual and often leads to personal questions, as we've already seen," she said.

"Ah, and getting to know each other is a bad idea, right?" he asked.

"Exactly."

"So, I'm thinking we'll advertise in the *Sacramento Bee* and on Facebook. You probably don't know if the program is already set up on social media, huh?"

Once she'd finished eating, Eve had spread out her planner on her side of the table, excited to share her ideas.

"We can even do an event page and people can RSVP online. We can post pictures and videos of the dogs and their handlers—Oh!"

"Watch out, ladies and gentlemen, she has an idea," Oliver said.

"Ha-ha, but yes I do! Alpha's dogs come from the local shelter, right?"

"I believe so," he said.

"So, we could use the bachelor auction as a chance for adoptable animals to be seen by the public. The shelter can sign up their dogs, and the trainers from the program can lead the dogs out. I'll look into a vendor who sells homemade dog treats, and we can stuff picnic baskets with both dog and people food. People can bid on a 'picnic with a pooch' and the pooch's handler. They'll get to know the dog and have one free training lesson. You could have the trainers teach the winners some basic skills. I think it could work!"

"You're not talking about the kids, right?" he asked.

"No, the adult trainers. The kids can walk the Alpha dogs around the event, handing out information and doing mini demonstrations."

"So, you're essentially pimping out the trainers, right? It's not really the dogs people are bidding on," he said.

Eve paused for half a second before answering. It was true that the auction's main focus was the dogs, but if they got enough attractive male and female trainers? Well, if the rest of them looked anything like Oliver Martinez, women would pay extra to spend an afternoon with the trainers.

"I mean, if you want us to strut our stuff for charity, you could at least be up-front about it," he said.

"It's about the dogs, but if someone happens to notice how good-looking one of the trainers is and wants to pay a little more, then I say yay."

"I feel objectified," he said.

Eve burst out laughing. "Does it make you uncomfortable to have people ogling your hot body?"

"You think my body is hot, huh?" he teased.

Well, hadn't she just veered away from professional and dived into outrageous? Yet despite the dangerous turn of the conversation, she couldn't seem to stop talking. "Please, you know you're nice to look at."

"Why, I think that is the nicest thing you've said to me since we met," he said.

"What?" Eve twisted her face in an expression of mock horror. "You mean in the hour that I've known you, I've only paid you *one* compliment? How dare I?"

Oliver's deep chuckle made her smile along with him. If she was being honest with herself, she'd actually been having fun sparring with him. He was confident, funny, and didn't back down just because of who her dad was.

Which made it dangerously easy to like him.

Liking him was fine, even being friendly with him. But she'd also caught herself gazing too long into his eyes and admiring the little crinkles in the corners when he smiled. His mouth was perfect, neither too full nor too thin, and when his tongue slipped across his lips to catch the sprinkles of salt from his french fries, she'd caught herself doing the same, imagining that tongue on hers. His big, tan hands looked rough, and she could almost feel them trailing across her skin, leaving lightning strikes of desire in their wake.

Stop it, now! He is not the first military man you've thought was hot, and he won't be the last.

Their server came back to the table with their check, and Eve reached into her purse for her wallet, but Oliver laid some cash down.

"What are you doing? I can pay for my meal," she said.

"It's okay, I've got it."

"But this isn't a date," she said, ignoring the definite squeak in her voice.

"I know that, but it doesn't mean I can't buy your lunch."

Eve pulled out a ten-dollar bill. "I'll leave the tip, then."

"It's just easier if I add it to the bill," he said firmly. He stood up to go pay at the front and added, "If you're nice to me, I might let you pay next time."

He walked away, and Eve started to gather up her papers, surprised and confused. Most of the time, guys expected her to split the bill with them on dates, and yet Oliver had snatched it up for a business meeting.

Before she joined him in the front of the restaurant, she caught the server and slipped her the ten. "Thank you."

"Thank *you*," the server said.

They walked out the door, and Eve saw Oliver shaking his head.

"What?"

"Nothing, just that between the two of us, she made a twenty-dollar tip on a twenty-three-dollar meal," he said.

Back at the car, Eve unlocked the door with a laugh. "Well, at least we made her day better."

"You would have made a lousy soldier," Oliver said teasingly.

Despite his lighthearted tone, Eve bristled. "Why do you say that?"

"Because every time I've tried to take the lead on something, you go your own way," he said.

Though he wasn't wrong, his assumption grated on her and reminded her of her dad, telling her when she was fifteen that she needed to stop worrying about guns and shooting ranges and concentrate on more important things, like grades and getting ready for college. The one time she'd mentioned the military, he'd laughed and told her she was too bullheaded, that she couldn't even follow her soccer coach's instructions.

To be fair, that coach had been an idiot.

"Ironically, that's something my dad and you have in common," she said.

"Thinking you're too independent for the military? Is that a bad thing?" Strapping himself into his seat, he added, "I bet you were the rebel girl who wore 'Question Authority' T-shirts and turned down every dumb jock who asked you out."

"There you go making an ass out of yourself by assuming you know me," she said. Eve started the car and backed up before continuing. "Actually, I played soccer and never got so much as detention. And I dated at least two football players, but they weren't stupid."

"Huh, well look at that. You were straightlaced, and I was the guy your daddy warned you about."

Eve merged into traffic and asked, "What kind of guy was that?"

"Let's just say my mom had to have more than one talk with the principal, and my dad, who was a cop, didn't appreciate having to bury pending charges when I got arrested."

"What did you get arrested for?" she asked.

"Joyriding with my friends," he said. "I grew up in small-town Texas, and I rode shotgun while my best friend boosted a car with three other guys. We'd been drinking a bit, and when we came around a turn, there was a cow in the road. Kenny swerved, and boom, we hit a pole head-on and had to call my dad. We were idiots. We could have all been killed, but as it was, we escaped with minor injuries and community service, but

Kenny... Well, Kenny was driving, so he went to jail and I went into the military."

The small voice in her head warned her to hold her tongue, but she hadn't listened so far today. Why start now?

"You were lucky. I mean, it's terrible about your friend, but drinking and driving is idiotic on its own *without* stealing a car."

"I know that. The only reason we got off as light as we did is because my dad was friends with the car's owner and he spoke up for us," he said. "If I had driven, it could have easily been me in Kenny's place."

"Have you talked to Kenny since?" she asked.

"Not in years," Oliver said.

Silence stretched in the car until Oliver admitted, "I have no idea why I told you that."

"Because we were talking about who we were in high school." They were complete opposites; that was for sure. She had always played it safe, hadn't even had her first drink until she was twenty-one. Not that she hadn't had the chance, but she calculated risks, always had. Her mom used to call her the "cautious one," while her brother was the wild one. Even her few rebellions had been small.

"Yeah, well, I would have been one of those idiots you wouldn't have dated," Oliver said.

Eve thought about that. There had been guys who'd gotten into trouble at her school, and she remembered rolling her eyes at them, thinking they were morons. No, sixteen-year-old her would definitely have steered clear of Oliver.

"Just for the record, I don't drink and drive," he said.

"That's good to know."

When they reached the program facility, Eve parked and turned off the car. "So, I have a photographer friend who can come out this week and take pictures of the dogs and handlers. Do you think two on Saturday afternoon will work?"

"I'll have to talk to Sparks and the rest of the guys, but there shouldn't be a problem," he said.

"Good. I'd also like to get pictures of the facility. I know this place just opened a month ago, but shots of the kids working with the dogs would be great. I want to have the social-media pages and website up by next Monday, if they aren't up already. I can show you how to tweak them if you need help."

"Wait, me?" he asked.

"Yeah, you. You're helping me, and I have other things to take care of, so you're in charge of the program's public image."

"I barely have a Facebook page," he said.

"Welcome to the modern age," she said.

Oliver opened the car door with a rueful smile. "Why me?"

"Maybe this will teach you not to get into bar fights," she said, her mouth twitching with humor.

He groaned, and before she realized what she was doing, she grabbed his hand. "Hey, thanks for lunch. By the way, can I see your phone?"

"Why, so you can put your number in it?"

Her eyes shot up to meet his, but he looked just as surprised as she felt.

"Actually, yes, since we'll be working so closely together," she said softly.

Oliver handed Eve his phone, and she released his hand. He leaned over to watch her fingers fly over the screen as she entered her number.

When she finished, she handed it back to him. "Call me when you find out about the dogs."

Oliver took the phone, but before she could pull away, he caught her hand. His grip shifted, and he brought the back of it to his mouth, pressing a soft kiss there. "I'll call you soon."

Eve's insides turned to Jell-O, and she said nothing as he released her hand and got out of her car. Tingles still lit her skin on fire, and she lightly ran her thumb across the place where he'd kissed her. She could still feel the warmth of his mouth.

Chapter Four

FIVE DAYS LATER, Oliver stood in the kennels in the back of the facility. There were twenty-five chain link kennels lining the far end of the laminate floor, and although most were empty, there were a few large dogs barking and whining at him, including several shepherds and Labrador mixes, breeds he recognized. Sparks had told him that while the kids were there training, the dogs slept in crates in their bunks. This handful of dogs were the only ones that hadn't been assigned yet.

Sparks stopped in front of the last kennel. "Oliver, this is Beast. You'll be training him."

Oliver looked through the kennel gate, saw the huge brown dog, and scowled. The mutt had a wrinkly, flat face, and his large body rippled with muscle as he stood up. After a long, lazy stretch, he slowly loped over to the front of the kennel. Oliver had spent the week working with several of the kids from Best's group and their dogs, but up until now, he'd avoided having to train one himself.

Oliver had told Sparks about the dog auction and their involvement, and Sparks had protested until Oliver had told him that Eve's father was the general. Unless he wanted to end up on the general's shit list, too, Oliver had suggested that Sparks pull up his big-boy panties and deal.

It wasn't like Oliver wasn't going to be up on the stage with him. Eve had come up with a detailed plan for the event with duties for everyone, and she hadn't missed a beat. All of the head trainers would be leading out a shelter dog for the "Picnic with a Pooch" auction and after lunch would give the winner one basic lesson in obedience training. The kids would be leading their dogs around the facility with raffle tickets to sell for several large prizes Eve was collecting. Oliver had actually been relieved at how easy the gig at Alpha Dog had been so far.

Then this morning, Sparks had informed Oliver that Best had found just the right dog for him to work with, and he couldn't wuss out now. He had told Best he would help train dogs and work with the kids while he was here, so he wasn't about to go back on his word.

Even if he was pretty sure Best was using the ugly dog to mess with him again. He should never have admitted that he wasn't a big fan of dogs.

"Do you have anything with less drool? Why can't I have one of the Labs?" Huge-ass dogs with massive jaws and saliva hanging from their lips hadn't been what he had in mind to train.

Sparks opened the kennel and attached a leash to Beast's collar. "Nope, just Beast. He's been at the shelter for several months; people kept passing him by because of his size and looks, but with a bit of training, he'll make a great military or police dog. Best said he would be a good match for you, since you're both stubborn sons of bitches."

"What am I supposed to do with him?"

"Take him home with you. I take Dilbert home." Dilbert was Sparks's canine charge, a huge black-and-white pit bull that liked to stick his face in Oliver's crotch. "Best temperament-tested him before he brought him over, so he should be shiny. Oh, but he did say that they are transitioning him onto the program's diet, so he might be a little gassy."

Best *would* set him up with a giant slobbering fart factory. "I'm going to kick that guy's ass."

Sparks slapped the leash into Oliver's hand. "Do what you gotta do, but I am going to grab Dilbert and get the rest of the guys ready for this photo shoot."

At the mention of the shoot, Oliver's skin hummed with anticipation. He hadn't seen Eve since Monday, but they had talked on the phone. She'd called on Tuesday to find out about the dog's temperaments, and when he'd confirmed they were good to go, she'd been off and running. The first thing she'd wanted to do was get the pictures taken, and Saturday was the only day that worked for all of the trainers.

After the shoot, they were going to go over her massive to-do list and use the pictures to set up the social-media accounts. But all Oliver cared about was getting to see her again, since he hadn't been able to get her off his mind all week. Especially since she was texting and calling several times a day to ask his opinion or add something else to the list of things they needed to get done.

The doors that led to the back training field crashed open, and a group of teenaged boys walked in. Jorge Ortiz, one of the kids Oliver had taken off Best's hands, shouted, "Hey, yo, Sergeant Martinez! That is one ugly ass dog!"

"I'm sure he was thinking the same thing about you, Ortiz," Oliver said.

The kid's face flushed, and the guys around him started in, razzing him about his looks, but he smiled good-naturedly. Ortiz was the quintessential class clown who had just been in the wrong place at the wrong time smoking pot with his friends. He'd actually confided to Oliver that being in the bunks was better than being home with his mom, who was scary as shit.

Of the three kids assigned to Oliver, he had to admit that Ortiz was his favorite. There had been an instant bond with the teenager, while his other two charges were a bit more damaged. Tommy Drake was a skinny white kid of fifteen with a chip the size of Antarctica on his shoulder, and Darrel Quinn was a towering black kid who hardly said a word. Oliver knew just looking into the kid's dark eyes that he had seen some shit, and he'd mentioned to Sparks that Darrel might need someone to talk to. Someone who had come out of hairy situations and could relate to what was going on inside the kid.

"So, when is the general's daughter supposed to stroll in here to crack the whip?' Sparks asked.

"Eve's supposed to be here with the photographer in half an hour," Oliver said.

"Eve, huh?" Sparks smirked at him.

"What, it's her name," he said.

"And yet Best was ordered to call her Ms. Reynolds," Sparks said.

"It's just because we're working together," Oliver said. In actuality, he'd never asked her if he could call her Eve, but somehow, he didn't think she'd mind.

"Well, when *Eve* gets here, send her out back. Figured we'd set up in the training yard, since it's such a nice day and it's the only place where the grass is green."

Sparks walked away from Oliver, leaving him alone with the monster at his feet. The dog stopped panting long enough to shake his head, sending long streams of slobber flying in every direction, several of which stuck to Oliver's pant leg. He grunted in disgust.

"You have problems, pal."

"Well, if that isn't the pot calling the kettle black," a woman said behind him.

Oliver looked up as Eve came up alongside him decked out in black slacks and a sheer polka-dot blouse. Her hair was loose around her shoulders, and those same sexy glasses slid down the bridge of her nose as she glanced at Beast with a smile. "And who are you, big guy?"

Beast's whole body started to tremble, and then he was on his feet, every muscle working to make him wiggle as he approached Eve.

Oliver pulled back, warning, "Watch out, he's a mess."

Eve laughed, and to Oliver's surprise, she knelt down in her slacks and held out her hand to Beast. "Are you a mess? Huh?"

Her soft, cajoling tone made Beast pull harder, and Oliver relaxed enough to let the dog nuzzle her fingers. She ran her palm across his broad head, rubbing his floppy ears. With a groan, Beast sank to the floor, leaning into her massaging hand.

Eve let out a husky laugh, and when she looked up, Oliver couldn't look away from those shiny green eyes.

"He is a serious ham," she said. "We had a big dorky dog when I was a kid, but after Moose died, my mom wanted a Pomeranian. I want to get a dog, but my apartment doesn't allow more than one animal and I already have a cat."

Oliver watched her, transfixed by her relaxed, playful manner. He wasn't paying attention to Beast, who had managed to climb onto Eve's lap.

"Shit, I am sorry," Oliver said. He was about to yank the dog away when she wrapped her arms around Beast and laughed again, kissing the big ugly dog on his head.

The click of a camera drew Oliver's attention to a lanky guy taking pictures of Eve as she cuddled Beast.

"Okay, come on." Oliver pulled the dog off her and groaned when he saw the mass of short brown hair covering her clothes. "I'm sorry."

Eve climbed to her feet and brushed at the hair. "It's okay, it just means you know my secret."

"You like dogs?" He couldn't help staring at her. Her sheer joy made him want to let Beast loose again to draw another one of those full-bodied laughs from her.

"No, that I don't mind getting dirty," she said.

Oliver knew Eve had no idea how her words affected him, and he tried to cover up the raw lust heating his body as he thought about all the dirty things he'd love to do with her.

"Caleb, come meet Sergeant Oliver Martinez and his dog…"

"Beast," Oliver said.

Caleb put the camera back in his bag and held his hand out to Oliver. "Pleased to meet you. Evie said you two are planning this thing together." Caleb leaned forward and whispered, "My advice is to just smile, nod, and do whatever she wants. She can be a pistol when she doesn't get her way."

Evie? Oliver squeezed Caleb's hand, a niggling of jealousy worming through his brain. Caleb's advice was too intimate.

"Good to meet you." Releasing Caleb's hand, Oliver turned to Eve and said, "Sparks is setting everyone up out back for the pictures. Figured if you wanted some shots of the guys training the dogs, it was the best place to do it," he said.

"Great. I ordered special jackets for the dogs to wear during the event—with cargo pockets. Easier to carry the money from the raffle tickets. Oh, and I want to talk to Sparks about setting up a demonstration at the event. I'm thinking we could show what the dogs are actually trained to do. It would be exciting. I've actually contacted a few of the local high schools to see if we can set up there for everything. I just think it would be easier to use their gym, auditorium, and campus, instead of having to set up fences and rent bleachers."

"Hey, you're the boss," Oliver said.

"Man, do not encourage her," Caleb said, earning a sour look from Eve that twisted Oliver's guts up.

"Sounds like you know her pretty well," Oliver said. Had either of them noticed his sharp tone?

Apparently not, because Caleb just laughed. "Our parents have been friends for a long time, and she used to constantly bug me to play *Clueless* and go to movies with her. She didn't give a rip that I was a dude; she still tried to make me play Dion."

"Oh, come on, you loved it. And if I hadn't kept you around, you never would have met your wife," Eve said.

"It's true. I'm actually married to Evie's best friend, Jenny, who played Ty," Caleb said. "I owe Evie everything, so I also tend to say, 'whatever she wants.'"

"That's because you're a smart man," Eve said.

Oliver knew it was stupid to be relieved, but he couldn't help it. The thought of Eve with anyone else grated on him, even though he knew he was playing with fire thinking about her as anything more than a means to get back in the field. Wrecking his career over a woman would be beyond moronic. And despite his reaction to her, a few hours of hot, world-rocking sex wasn't worth derailing everything he'd worked for.

Too bad his logic was being overruled by every other cell in his body.

"I'm gonna get some other shots of the place, so I'll talk to you all later," Caleb said.

Caleb took off, leaving Oliver alone with Eve, who was rummaging through her purse. When she pulled out a lint roller and started running it along her curves, his mouth dried up.

"Is it all gone?"

Oliver realized Eve was talking to him. "What?"

"Did I miss any?" she asked, turning this way and that. As she spun around, Oliver couldn't stop himself from eyeballing her ass in those simple black slacks.

"I think you're good." Oliver met her gaze as she turned back around. A black eyelash rested on her cheek, and Oliver reached out to pick it up before she could move. Holding it up for her, he said, "Make a wish."

Before she could blow, sharp pain erupted down his shin, and Oliver hollered, jumping back. He bent over and lifted his pant leg to find four red abrasions on his shin where Beast had dragged his beefy paw. The dog had placed himself between Eve and Oliver, and Oliver got the feeling the dog was claiming her.

"It's on, Fido. I just became your worst nightmare," Oliver said too low for anyone else to hear.

Beast snorted, snot flying and smacking Oliver in the face.

Oliver stood up with his eyes closed, the cool wet snot sitting on his eyelids. He was just about to drag his T-shirt over his face, when he felt Eve touch his cheek. Before he could move, she was wiping his face with something cold and wet, starting with his eyelids.

"I keep wipes in my purse for when I spill things, which happens about five times a day. I'm one of those people who looks really responsible and put together, but in reality, I'm a mess." Oliver opened his eyes, watching her as she cleaned him up and continued talking. "I mean, you should see what I carry around. People always joke about everything women carry in their purses, but I am prepared for every disaster."

As she rambled on, Oliver became aware that he had bent closer to help her reach his face. He inhaled the light, floral scent of her perfume and sweetness that seemed to be all Eve. It was bliss and torture at the same time, having her close enough to touch and taste, yet being denied the pleasure.

When he couldn't take it any longer, Oliver caught her wrist as she wiped along his cheek. "I can finish up."

Eve's cheeks lit up red and she pulled away, holding the wet wipe out to him. "Sorry, I just thought you got some in your eye and was trying to help."

"I know," he said, taking the wipe.

After a moment of awkward silence, Eve said, "I guess I should go make sure that Caleb is getting everything. We need to discuss the social-media stuff after the photo shoot, so don't take off, okay?"

"I won't," he said.

As she walked away, Beast whimpered, and Oliver frowned down at the dog. "Look, we're stuck with each other. She is not going to save you, so you might as well forget about her. She's not for you."

And definitely not for me.

Beast grunted, as if he was disagreeing with Oliver. But even if Eve did want Oliver back, she would be his downfall. She might be stubborn and outspoken, but she was also too nice for her own good. He'd never had nice, didn't even know what to do with it. The women he went for knew the score and never asked for more than he could give.

And no matter how many naughty thoughts he might have about her, Evelyn Reynolds was a woman who wanted it all. She'd demand everything from him, and if he couldn't deliver...

He couldn't take the chance that she might ruin him.

"No. She is definitely not for us."

"So, YOU READY to work?" Oliver asked several hours later.

Eve wanted to say yes, but the pictures had taken longer than she'd expected and she was so hungry she was ready to eat a horse.

"Sure. Do you want to do this in that conference room?" They stood in the front lobby beside Beast, who sat panting at Oliver's side. Everyone else was eating dinner in the large dining hall, and although Sparks had invited her to join them, she'd actually wanted to be alone with Oliver so they could get their work done.

But it was almost too quiet around them, making the loud, rapid thud of her heart that much louder. She was still embarrassed at having practically molested him earlier, but she had to work with him, which meant shoving down her attraction to him. No more touching, flirting, teasing—nothing.

"Yeah, but at the risk of you getting pissed, I'm pretty hungry," he said. "Maybe we could order a pizza or something?"

Eve's stomach rumbled at the thought. "I would love some pizza."

Oliver pulled out his cell phone and dialed. Before she could pick it up, he reached out and grabbed her bulky laptop bag, waving at her to follow him. "Yeah, I'd like to order a large..." He paused, looking at her.

"I like pepperoni and olive," she said.

"Pepperoni and olive pizza, a two liter of Coke, and add some of those cheesy breadsticks...eight of them, with marinara and ranch. Yeah, delivery." As Oliver led her into a small room with a rectangular table and several chairs, he set down her bag and rattled off the address and his credit card number.

Eve took a seat, watching him end the call, and her gaze was drawn to the tan, sinewy muscles of his arm.

"Are you mad?" Oliver set his cell on the table and sat down next to her. She shifted her chair a bit away from him, trying to put some distance between them.

Damn, why does he have to smell so good?

"About what?" she asked.

"That I didn't let you pay for the pizza. I didn't even ask if you liked Round Table; it's just what I always order 'cause I live right down the street."

"No, that's fine," she said.

Suddenly, Beast was pushing his way between their chairs, and Oliver cursed. "Will you get out of the way?"

"For a guy who's supposed to be training dogs, you don't seem like much of a dog person," she said.

"My dad worked with German shepherds and rottweilers as police dogs, so I was around them, but we never had one as a pet."

"That's too bad," Eve said, reaching down to stroke Beast's big head. "Dogs are awesome. I bet if you gave this guy a chance, you'd love him."

"He's pushy," Oliver groused.

"Ah, you don't like him because he's like you." Eve grinned as Oliver glared at her.

"So, this social-media stuff. Tell me what you want me to do," he said.

Eve pushed her irritation down at his brusqueness. What had happened to the guy who'd tried to charm her over lunch? Or the one who'd looked at her earlier with so much heat, she almost combusted just being near him? Had that all just been one-sided? Had she imagined it?

What does it matter? Didn't we already decide that getting involved with him was a bad idea? That we weren't going to be ruled by sexual attraction?

Shaking off her hurt, she took out the laptop to show him her spreadsheet. "Okay, I took the liberty of setting up your website domain, your Facebook, Twitter, and Instagram, since your guys hadn't done it yet."

"Hey, why do I get lumped in with the rest of these guys? I just got here."

"Because I saw your Facebook page, and you really are barely there." Shit, she had just admitted to cyber stalking him. Great.

"You checked me out, huh?"

"Don't get too excited," she said. "I wanted to show you the basics of how to get in and out of the accounts, set up events, and post. Do you have the apps on your phone?"

"No, like I said, I barely look at my personal Facebook account," Oliver said.

She sighed loudly and held out her hand. "Give it."

"Has anyone told you you're bossy?"

"All the time, but it tends to be effective when I want things to get done," she said.

Oliver picked up his phone and held it out to her. Just as she was about to take it, he pulled it back. "First, say please."

"Really?" She sounded exasperated, but that was too bad.

"You want my phone *and* my help? Then I'm going to need you to have a little patience and treat me with respect. Understood?"

He could tell he'd surprised her by her wide-eyed, horror-filled expression. After several seconds she flushed crimson and looked away from him.

"I'm sorry. I was rude. May I please have your phone?"

"Thank you." He placed the phone in her hand and watched as she bent over the screen, noting that her cheeks were still a dull red. He got the feeling that Eve didn't get called out on being anything but nice too often, but he didn't want Eve to think he was weak and that she could just run roughshod over him and he would sit back and take it. She was a strong, independent, sexy woman, but he was a man. A strong, virile man who didn't cow or bow to anyone.

When she finished downloading the apps, he reached out to take her hand. Her soft, warm skin against his rough palm was irresistible, and he couldn't stop from running his thumb across the back of it as he studied her nails. Each one had a different design. At first, she tried to tug her hand away, but when he held it firm, she relaxed. Slightly.

"Live, Love, Laugh, Repeat," he read aloud. The words were staggered in black across the white nail polish. "I like it."

"Do you want me to bring you a catalog next time?" The laughter lacing her tone was a little shaky, and he wondered if his touch made her nervous or if she was still put out with him.

"Catalog?" he said, bewildered. He looked up from her nails and met her gaze, the green of her eyes sparkling behind her glasses. His hand tightened on hers, and he started to lean in.

"For the nails. It's a press-on thing." Her words were nearly breathless, and he was sure she'd leaned into him, too, her mouth opening slightly.

Oliver reached up, his fingers itching to tangle in her loose, dark hair...

"Whoa, am I interrupting something?" an amused voice asked from the doorway.

Oliver clenched his fist as his gaze swung to Best lounging in the doorway, grinning. Oliver wanted to drag him outside and knock that smirk off his face, but Eve nearly jumped out of her seat.

"Actually, I forgot I had plans tonight, and I'm already late," Eve said, turning off and closing up her laptop. She put it away before swinging the laptop bag over her shoulder. "I'll post the pictures tomorrow. If you can take photos and videos throughout the week and upload them to the program page, that would be great. And if you have any trouble with posting media, let me know and I'll be in touch. But don't post more than five times a day, unless it's important."

"Evelyn, wait." Oliver stood up and tried to reach for her, but she eluded him, her color high. She was out of reach and out the door before he could stop her.

Oliver glared at Best. "Has anyone ever told you that you have shit timing?"

"What? You should be thanking me," Best said.

"And why is that?"

"Because I just saved you from an agonizing death at the hands of General Reynolds. If he found out you were making a move on his daughter..."

Oliver knew what he meant. If he got involved with Evelyn, he could kiss his career and his dick good-bye.

Chapter Five

On Sunday afternoon, Eve was curled up on the couch watching *The Walking Dead*, but she wasn't really paying attention. Since last night, all she'd been able to do was replay that moment with Oliver, the one where he'd been two seconds away from planting those delicious-looking lips on hers. His eyelids had been heavy, already starting to close, and that hand had been coming up to her face, probably to cup it. Both had sent her pulse racing so fast she'd actually been a little dizzy.

Eve flopped onto her side, groaning. Her cat, Matilda, who'd been comfortably laying across her lap, meowed and stood up, her back arching as she stretched.

"Sorry, babe, but mommy's having a moment over here," Eve said.

Matilda's yellow eyes were unsympathetic as she twitched her fluffy black tail.

Eve reached out to rub Matilda's ears, attempting to pacify her. As the cat leaned into her ministrations and purred loudly, Eve's mind drifted back to Oliver. Last night, when he'd called her out for being rude, she'd been horrified that he'd been right. She had been trying to put some distance between them, and her best defense was a "brick wall of superiority"—as her freshman science partner had told her once. Like her father, she had the ability to lead people, but it didn't always make her a fan favorite.

Oliver had known what she was doing and yet, he'd just accepted her apology and moved on. Hell, if Best hadn't walked in, he would have kissed her.

And there was not a doubt in her mind that she would have let him.

She knew he wasn't right for her, even for a brief fling, but she also couldn't deny that she wanted him.

Bad.

And she hated it. Obsessing over a guy was something she'd thought she'd outgrown, yet here she was, unable to get the loaded question out of her head...

What would've happened if we hadn't been interrupted?

Their kiss could have been a dud, and working with him would have become awkward as ass until they got over it and realized they'd dodged a bullet.

Somehow she doubted it, though. Just Oliver holding her hand was enough to light her up. She'd spent the better part of last night imagining his lips and hands all over her body, driving her crazy until she exploded.

Then she'd started worrying about what would happen after the mind-blowing sex—sex that was so amazing, she actually threw out her vibrator and locked him in her closet, only to take him out whenever she wanted him.

Okay, that one was on the crazy side, but a girl could dream, right?

Once the sex and newness wore off, she'd still want the nice, normal, home-every-night guy, and eventually, their affair would crash and burn. It was inevitable and better to put the kibosh on it before it started.

A knock on her door jolted her out of her head, and Eve bolted upright. Her friends knew how she spent every Sunday: catching up on shows and vegging out until dinner with her parents at six. And even if they needed something, they would have called first.

Matilda jumped off the couch and scrambled into the other room as Eve stood up.

"Who is it?" she called.

"It's your father, Evelyn, open the door."

"Shit," she said aloud.

"I heard that," he said.

Curse these cheap apartments and their thin doors.

Glancing around her disastrous apartment, she started gathering last night's take-out containers and rushing to the kitchen to throw them away. "Hang on."

"There is no need to clean up. I've been your father for twenty-five years," he said. Eve could hear the amusement in his tone, but despite his words, she knew if she answered the door right now—in yoga pants, an oversized sweatshirt, and her hair falling out of a messy ponytail—he wouldn't be able to help commenting.

"Evelyn, now," he barked, making her feel like a six-year-old who didn't want to leave the playground.

"Fine, but I really don't want to hear it, Dad," she said.

She opened the door, and her father stepped past her into the apartment. She watched his eyes shift around the room and knew what he was thinking as he took in her sink piled with dishes, her clothes thrown about the floor and furniture, and the dust gathered across every surface.

"Eve—"

"Bububububu…I don't want to hear it," she repeated.

Her dad's mouth thinned under his thick silver and black mustache. Eve wasn't sure why mustaches and beards had started coming back the last few years, but she had to admit that the look fit her father's tan, weathered face. Dressed in a collared shirt, jeans, and a cap with an American flag on the front, he looked like a laid-back man enjoying his day off, but Eve knew better. Her dad never relaxed.

"So, what brings you by?" she asked.

Her father walked over to her arm chair, flicking one of her bras off the back of it before sitting down. "You mother wanted me to come by and check on you. She was concerned when you called to say you weren't coming over for dinner."

Eve refrained from rolling her eyes. When she had told her mother that she'd just needed a day to relax, her mom had been cool about it.

Which meant her dad was here because he was worried about her. How sweet.

"Do you want some coffee?" Eve asked. She'd gotten up this morning and been lazing on the couch, but if she was going to have a coherent conversation with her dad, she needed caffeine.

"Do you have a mug that's clean?" he asked.

Eve slammed a cupboard and held up the black mug she kept just for him. "You just can't help it, can you?"

"No, I can't. Not when you're living in a pigsty and you look like—"

"Let me stop you there," Eve said. "My apartment might not look like a *Better Homes and Gardens* magazine, but it is hardly a pigsty." Pausing to start the coffeemaker, she turned and pinned him with a hard look. "And you should definitely know better than to insult a woman's appearance."

"You're still my daughter, and it's my job to tell you that a man wants a woman who takes pride in her appearance," he said.

Eve's skin prickled with heat as anger flashed through her body. "I am put together six days a week. If on my one day off I want to wear sweats and not brush my hair, then that is my right. A right I should thank you for, by the way."

"I did not fight for your right to look like a slob," he barked.

Eve took a breath, arched her back, and cracked her neck, attempting to banish the urge to tell her father to get out. "Dad, why don't you tell me why you're really here and stop pussyfooting around?"

Surprisingly, her dad didn't comment on her language and instead got right to the point. "How has Martinez been working out?"

Eve hesitated. "Sergeant Martinez is good."

"Really? He hasn't tried getting out of the fund-raiser at all?"

"No, he's been a big help," Eve said. Suspicion overwhelmed her. "Was that your plan? For me to report back to you on this guy if he didn't fall in line?"

"I don't have a plan, I was just asking a question," he said casually.

Too casually.

"Why don't I believe you?" she asked.

"There's no reason why you shouldn't."

"I know that Oliver is the guy who kicked Hank's ass a few weeks ago. This wouldn't be about avenging the family honor or something stupid like that, would it?"

Her dad watched her thoughtfully, and Eve squirmed. The last thing she wanted was for her dad to know she liked Oliver.

Whoa, when did attraction turn to like?

"I am not petty, Evelyn. *Oliver* was taken off MP active patrol because he was fighting with a civilian off base and I wanted to make an example of him."

Shit, he'd noticed she'd dropped Oliver's name.

Eve's phone went off in the nick of time, blaring Meghan Trainor's "All about That Bass." She looked around for it and saw it on the coffee table next to her dad. Before she'd even taken a step, he picked it up and looked at the front.

His expression was blank, but when he held the phone out to her, his tone was cutting. "Speak of the devil."

Eve nearly groaned out loud, then snatched the phone. "Hello?"

"Hey, Evelyn, it's Oliver."

"Hi. You know, it's really not a good time."

"I don't want to keep you, I just wanted to apologize for last night. I was out of line and I just wanted to let you know that I will be on my best behavior from now on."

"That's great, why don't we go over those ideas later on today, okay?" She hoped to God her dad hadn't heard Oliver's apology; she definitely didn't want him to start asking questions. Especially when it was nothing. Less than nothing.

"Huh? You want to meet up today?" He sounded so adorably confused.

"Yeah, I'll text you the details in a bit, but I've got to go, okay?"

"Okay—"

Eve hung up and went back to preparing the coffee.

"Evelyn," her dad said behind her.

"Yeah?" She turned and caught the deadly look on his face.

"I've always thought you had a good head on your shoulders and, besides that one hiccup when you were a kid, were an excellent judge of character," he said.

That hiccup had been Andy Briggs when she was seventeen. Her father had never liked him, but she'd fallen hard for the blue-eyed army private, only to find out he was playing her. And once her father found out, he'd managed to have Andy transferred, but he'd never let Eve forget about it.

"Thank you? Why do I hear a big 'but' coming?"

"*But*, I am worried about Sergeant Martinez taking advantage of you—"

"Let me stop you there," Eve said, setting her cup down. "No one is going to take advantage of me, and there is nothing going on between me and Sergeant Martinez. We are just working together, that's it."

"I just worry that he isn't pulling his weight and is creating more work for you."

Eve finished doctoring her coffee and sat down on the couch. "Honestly, Dad, he has done everything I've asked and hasn't shirked his responsibilities once. You might want to lighten up and give him the benefit of the doubt. Besides, I've seen Hank when he's had a few, and I've been tempted to knock his ass out myself."

"I know exactly how difficult your brother can be, but it doesn't change anything. Sergeant Martinez should have known better."

Eve sighed. She wasn't going to win an argument with her dad about her brother. He might say that he knew Hank's faults, but her brother had always been able to get away with murder. Perks of being the baby and a boy, she supposed.

"Fine. Is this why you dropped by? To ask about how Sergeant Martinez was doing? And don't tell me it was because mom was worried, because I don't buy it."

He had just finished taking a drink of his coffee and set his mug down on the coffee table before answering. "I just wanted to check in with you. It's not as if we see each other anymore without family dinner, and when I learned you weren't coming, I wanted to find out why. Now I know."

Man, he was a master of the guilt trip, but underneath that, she heard exactly what he was trying to say: *I miss you.* Despite their innate ability to drive each other nuts, they were close and she missed him, too.

"I know I've been a little absent, but I just want to do a good job. It's hard networking and getting a new business off the ground," she said. "I promise, next Sunday I'll be there and you can pump me for all the information you want about Sergeant Martinez or anything else."

"I'll hold you to that," her dad said. "Just be careful with Martinez. Still waters run deep with that one, and I don't want you getting hurt."

Eve opened her mouth to defend Oliver but thought better of it. There was no point in fighting with her dad about a man she wouldn't ever see again once the event was over. Nothing was going to happen between Oliver and her before or after, so why bother getting her dad bent out of shape?

"I will. I promise."

Her dad nodded and stood up. "Well, I guess I'll leave you to clean up."

Eve rolled her eyes and followed her dad to the door. "You just had to get that last dig in, huh?"

"I'm your father. It's my job to encourage you."

OLIVER STOOD IN the middle of his living room, staring at the fluffy material that used to be inside his couch cushions and now blanketed the floor. Beast lifted his head from where he sat gnawing the side of his leather armchair, and when Oliver saw the white cotton caught in the dog's lips and teeth, he lost it.

"I was in the shower for twenty fucking minutes! How in the fuck did you do all this in twenty minutes?"

Why in the hell had he listened to Sparks and Best? The two of them had told him that socialization and bonding were an important part of training and that he needed to take the monster dog home with him to do that. Now, he wouldn't be surprised if it was all just a setup. Give him the defective, destructive dog and just sit back and laugh.

Beast panted at him for a second before his wrinkly face scrunched up and he sneezed, sending stuffing and snot flying through the air. Oliver grabbed the leash, planning on taking the dog back to the facility, but instead, he found himself running after Beast as the dog grabbed one of the throw pillows and skidded out of the room.

It wasn't just the damage to his furniture that had Oliver ready to send Beast packing. When he'd left the dog in the backyard last night, Beast had howled for hours until Oliver had brought him inside and shut him in the crate he'd taken from the facility. But that was worse. Finally, Oliver had given up and let the dog out of the cage, leaving him to wander around Oliver's bedroom. Oliver had finally fallen into an exhausted sleep and woke up spooning Beast in his bed.

The day had progressed from there to this moment, chasing a dog through his house right before Eve was supposed to arrive.

When she'd texted that she wanted to come by to iron out the event details, he'd picked up the place quickly before grabbing a shower. Now, he just wanted to tell her not to come, that they would have to plan for another day because he had a dog to annihilate.

Beast barked at him as he bounded across the bed, a definite spring in the dog's every bounce.

"You think this is funny? I'm not playing with you, dude."

Beast barked again, and when Oliver lunged, Beast took off, letting out a howl as someone knocked on the door.

"This isn't over," Oliver snapped. The dog launched himself on top of the ruined couch, barking out the window.

"Get your ass down," Oliver shouted as he threw the door open.

Evelyn stood on the other side, her hair pulled back in a simple ponytail. Her black-framed glasses were missing today, giving him an unobstructed view of her green eyes as they crinkled in amusement.

"Bad timing?" she asked.

"You could say that." Oliver held the door open for her, and some of his anger dissolved as his gaze traveled over her white peasant blouse and flowing navy skirt. The top gave him a tantalizing view of her breasts, and the little tie on the front teased him, taunting him to pull it and spread the cotton open, exposing her to his eyes and lips.

"Oh, wow, what happened here?" she asked.

"That fucking dog happened," he said, shooting *that dog* a murderous glare.

"What did you do, leave him alone for hours?"

"No," he said, pointing around the room, "this happened while I was in the shower."

"Really?" Eve sounded like she didn't believe him. Without another word, she dropped to her knees and held out her arms to Beast. "Come on, buddy. Come here."

The dog bounded to her, wiggling and licking wherever he could. She held her hand behind her, and Oliver gave her the leash. Once she had it hooked onto Beast's collar, she stood up with a mischievous smile. "I don't know why he gives you so much trouble."

"Oh, I'm sure Best put him up to it," Oliver grumbled.

"Ah, and he gets a kick out of messing with you, huh?"

"That's just because I've let it go until now, but the dude owes me a sofa and chair."

Eve laughed and held the leash out to him. "I wonder if maybe you two just got off on the wrong foot. Perhaps you should open your mind to the possibility that Beast has issues and this is his way of dealing with them."

Oliver took her advice with a healthy dose of skepticism. "What makes you think he has issues?"

"Well, for starters, he came from the animal shelter, so he's got to have some baggage. The question is was he turned in because he has behavioral problems and his previous owners just couldn't deal? Or were the owners jackasses who just didn't want him anymore?" Her tone was sad as she added, "If he was loved, it's easy to assume that he is confused and misses it."

Oliver studied Eve. Her dreamy, sweet expression tugged at his heart, and he wondered who she was thinking about. A loved one she missed? A past lover? A bitter rush of jealousy churned in his stomach. He didn't want to think about another man having even a sliver of Evelyn's affections. Not when he wanted them all to himself.

"How is it you seem to know so much about what he's feeling? Are you an event planner by day and dog psychic by night?" He had been trying to make a joke, but one look at her face told him he'd insulted her.

"I'm just making an observation," she said curtly.

"Hey." He reached out and touched her arm, turning her toward him. "I was just teasing you."

She remained silent, and he took her chin in his hand, tilting her gaze up to meet his. "Why does it always seem like I can never say the right thing to you?"

A small smile played across those bee-stung lips. "Maybe I make you nervous."

Oliver rubbed his thumb across her bottom lip, and her sharp, warm breath spread over his skin. "Oh, you definitely make me nervous."

"I do?" Her breathless question stirred his cock to life.

"Yeah, you do. I can't relax around you, not with the way you make me feel," he said.

"How is that?" Her tone was soft, and Oliver dipped his head, his mouth hovering over hers.

"Like I'm standing in the sunshine every time I'm near you," he said.

"Oh."

Oliver didn't give her a chance to escape this time and covered her mouth with his, groaning as the sweet taste of her overwhelmed him. His hands slid back to cradle the back of her head, and he buried his fingers in her hair, loosening her ponytail. A tiny sigh escaped her, and he took advantage, slipping his tongue between her parted lips, coming undone when her tongue tangled with his. He felt her hands grip his waist, pulling him tighter against her body, and he wanted more. Never had he gotten so caught up in one kiss. And never had he ignored every warning bell for a woman, but with Evelyn, it was like common sense went out the window and was replaced by uncontrolled passion.

Oliver felt something pushing between them and opened his eyes to look down at Beast, who was trying to use his giant head to separate them. Ignoring him, Oliver maneuvered them toward the couch, propelling Eve down onto the mangled leather.

The kiss broke long enough for Eve's eyes to pop open, and she giggled. "Somehow, I never imagined making out on a cloud of couch stuffing."

Oliver grinned down at her. "What can I say? I'm an original."

"You're definitely different," she said.

"Is that a compliment?" His lips found the pulse point behind her ear and he felt her heart race against his mouth.

"I think so."

"You don't sound sure," he murmured against her jaw.

"Probably 'cause I can't think while you're kissing me," she whispered.

His mouth brushed hers. "Want me to stop?"

"God, no."

Chapter Six

EVE GRABBED OLIVER'S shoulders and held on as his kiss sent her head spinning. Everything that would have normally had her coming back to reality, telling her to slow down or she'd regret it, melted away with each stroke of his tongue.

Oliver's hand slid to her waist, then up under the fabric of her shirt, and the skin-to-skin contact was hot as he skimmed his palm up her side. She knew where he was headed, and her nipples pebbled in anticipation, gooseflesh spreading over her body.

Suddenly, Oliver got heavier, and she pulled away, gasping for breath as she realized that Oliver was struggling above her and cursing.

"Get the fuck off me, you dumb ass!"

Eve craned her head, and if she'd been able to breathe, she'd have laughed.

Beast had jumped on top of Oliver's back and was now laying on him, giving new meaning to the term *dog pile*. Finally, Oliver rolled and both he and Beast landed on the ground. Eve turned on her side, holding her stomach as she exploded into giggles.

"Well, you were definitely right about him having issues," Oliver grumbled, sending her into another fit of laughter. Tears were leaking out of the corner of her eyes, and she couldn't seem to stop. At least she wouldn't need to add any saline to her eyes to lube up her contact lenses.

When she calmed down enough to speak, she wiped at her eyes and sat up. "How can you be mad at that face?" She looked at Beast's flat face and teased, "He just wanted to play, too."

Suddenly, Oliver's face was inches from hers. "The kind of play I had in mind definitely didn't involve him."

His words created a dull ache between her legs, sobering her. He said all the right things, made her crazy, and yet, doubt and caution were slowly outweighing her lust.

Her father had pretty much told her he didn't like Oliver, and despite how good she felt now, what would happen after they had satisfied this electric attraction? They still had the event in two weeks, and if anything went south between them, it would make things awkward.

And it *would* go south eventually, because as much as she wanted to deny it now, throw caution to the wind, and jump his bones, they could barely be around each other without insulting one another.

Clearing her throat, she got up from the couch and retrieved her bag. "Yes, well, we should really concentrate on the auction."

She started toward the kitchen table, but quick as lightening, he was on his feet and he caught her arm, his expression concerned. Maybe a little confused.

She was right there with him.

"Whoa, two seconds ago we were about to rip each other's clothes off, and now you're acting like you've got ice in your veins. What's going on? Did I say something to piss you off again?"

"No, you didn't piss me off. I'm just stating facts. We have to work together, at least for the next few weeks, so it's not a good idea to get too…intimate."

"Because you don't like me?"

She caught herself before she yelled no. "I didn't say that."

"So, you do like me." It was a statement—one that both irritated and embarrassed her.

"I will admit, I am attracted to you, but I don't know you well enough to like you." Eve walked around him to the table and started unloading her folders and iPad.

"So, what do you gotta know to determine if I'm likable?" he asked, sitting across from her.

Eve sighed. Loudly. "Oliver—"

"Have I mentioned I like the way you say my name?"

"Sergeant Martinez, I don't think—"

"Now, that's just cold, *dulzura*," he said.

"I am not your *honey*," she snapped, sitting down. He seemed surprised she'd understood, so she explained. "I took Spanish for four years in high school and had a summer break in Mexico. Now, can we please get this done? I want to get home before *The Walking Dead* comes on."

"Why don't you watch it here? I've got cable, and we could order that pizza we never got to eat."

Eve bit the inside of her cheek, nearly groaning in frustration. "Man, you just don't give up, do you?"

"No," he said firmly. Then he sat forward and caught her hand before she could pull it back. *"Quiero que seas mía."*

Eve's heart slammed in her chest as she silently translated his words.

I want you to be mine.

"Stop it." Her cheeks felt like they were on fire, and she jerked her hand away. "No pizza. No *Walking Dead* with you, and definitely no being yours."

Oliver's ocean blue eyes bore into hers until she had to look away, afraid he'd see that she wasn't as strong as she sounded.

"Okay, so I'm thinking we start off at ten and have the auction at eleven. We'll have games for the kids and bouncy houses as well as private vendors selling canine treats, accessories, veterinary services, etcetera. And there will be several other military organizations represented."

"All of that sounds good, but you never answered my question," Oliver said.

"Which one?"

"I asked what you needed to know to decide whether or not you like me."

"I-wanna-see-you-naked like you or like-you-as-a-friend like you?"

"Either," he said.

Eve looked up from her iPad, right into his eyes. *God, why did they have to be so pretty?* They made her want to tell him the truth—that she already liked him in a definite let's-get-fleshy kind of way.

But deep down, she knew it was time to nip this flirting in the bud. She needed to prove she was right and that their attraction was just that. They would never last in the long run, not without the same goals in life.

"What's your idea of a real relationship?"

He spluttered, which was exactly what she'd expected. Nothing freaked a guy out or threw him off his game like talking about his intentions.

"It's a simple question, unless you aren't the relationship type," she said.

Oliver let out an uncomfortable chuckle and rubbed a hand over his shaved head. "I don't know. I had a girlfriend in high school, but we mostly just watched TV and—"

"I get it, you had a *real connection*," Eve said.

"Look, I don't have a lot of time or chances to meet girls, unless it's at a bar, and most of them aren't looking for more than a night or two," he said. "But I guess if I was going to spend a lot of time with one person, we'd do regular stuff. Go to dinner, maybe a movie, and maybe vacation together."

"But those are just activities," Eve said. "What do you think makes a *relationship* real?"

"Jesus, I don't know. I guess it's just the way two people feel about each other and whether they can stand to spend the rest of their lives together."

"Romantic," she said.

"What? It's true. We all have bullshit, but when we just start seeing someone, we try to hide that bullshit until there's no going back. I mean, you've already seen that I can be a jackass, my people skills are shit, and dogs hate me. But if we'd met under normal circumstances, like I saw you sitting alone at the café or something, I'd have asked if I could join you and would have been on my best behavior."

"If you had come up to my table in your uniform, you wouldn't have sat down," Eve said bluntly.

Oliver's eyebrows shot up. "You got something about guys in the military?"

"I know I want a calm, predictable life, and you don't get that when you marry a career man."

"Wow, I can't believe you would say that, given who your dad is," Oliver said.

"Believe me, my dad wants me to get involved with a soldier even less that I do."

Oliver didn't say anything, but guilt and shame niggled at her.

Why do you need to be ashamed for how you feel and what you want out of life?

"It's not that I don't respect you or the other men and women who do what you do, but I want a man who will be home for dinner at a decent hour and not gone for years on end. I also refuse to date doctors, lawyers, or CEOs."

"Well, good to know that you don't care about money, either."

"Money doesn't make up for being alone," she said softly.

"Considering I'm the last guy you want to get involved with, I'll respect your wishes," he said. "I'll be completely professional from now on."

Eve swallowed the lump in her throat, and a large part of her wished she hadn't said anything. Oliver picked up the folder marked VENDORS and started perusing it, but she didn't believe he was really reading it. She'd hurt his feelings.

It's better to stop whatever this is now than to drag it out and get hurt later. It's better this way.

"WELL, I GUESS that's it, then," Oliver said.

Over the last two hours, they had hammered out every detail and divided every task.

And it had been painfully polite, just the way Eve had wanted it.

Her admission that she didn't date military men had pissed him off and, worse, presented him with a challenge. He had always been a stubborn son of a bitch, and if anyone ever told him he couldn't do or have something, he'd go out of his way to prove them wrong.

Evelyn had just waved a bright-ass red flag in his face, and all he wanted to do was chase it.

Chase her.

"Thanks for helping me bust through all this," Eve said.

"And with enough time to watch *The Walking Dead*." Oliver thought she winced, but he might have imagined it. He could tell by the way she'd acted earlier that she regretted telling him about her dating policy, but he'd just chalked that up to her nice nature. For all her sass and snark, Eve was a sweetheart.

When she had all her stuff gathered up, she paused and glanced around his house. "You know, I could help you clean up. If you want."

"That's okay, I can get it."

"I don't mind…"

"Really, Evelyn, I'm fine. You didn't hurt my feelings or anything. I'm a big boy," he said.

"I didn't offer because I felt bad," she said testily. "I offered because despite the terrible people skills, I *do* like you and think we could be friends."

Great. Already in the friend zone.

"I have friends."

"I'm sure you do, but how many of them would help you clean up your house?" she asked.

Oliver grinned sheepishly. "That would be none."

"Hmm, then it seems you could do worse than a friend like me," she said.

"You think so, huh?" Damn, it would be easier if he didn't like her. If she really was just some girl he'd met in a bar who was down to fuck and nothing else. But instead, she was beautiful and sweet as well as funny and surprising.

"Where are your trash bags?" she asked, breaking him out of his thoughts.

"Above the fridge." Oliver's gaze traveled down over her bottom to the hard calf muscles straining in her legs as she actually stood on tiptoe to reach the box of trash bags.

Unable to resist, he came up behind her and pressed against her back, grabbing the box with ease. He held it in front of her as he placed his mouth next to her ear. "Anytime you need me for those *hard-to-reach places*, let me know."

She shivered against him, but he was almost positive she wasn't cold. The temptation to push his luck was crazy, yet he backed off. She could deny there was something more between them if she wanted, but that didn't mean he wouldn't prove how wrong she was.

"I'll grab the broom and dustpan," he said.

Oliver went down the hall to grab them from the closet and turned around to find Eve bent over, her skirt accentuating her ass as she scooped up handfuls of white fluff and avoided Beast's affections. Oliver gritted his teeth, cursing the raging hard-on he seemed to sport constantly whenever Eve was around.

"You are definitely going to want a new couch," she said.

"Yeah, well, I was due for one anyway before Cujo decided to use it as a chew toy," he said. Oliver concentrated on sweeping up excess fluff from the hardwood floor and ignoring Eve's round, gorgeous behind. He knew that her dating policy was meant to put him off. Whether she really didn't want to get involved or she was just afraid, he wasn't sure. Unfortunately, it hadn't worked, not with her staying to help clean up a mess she had nothing to do with.

"It sounds like Beast was just trying to help you out. Get you motivated."

Oliver shot her a glower and he loved that she laughed at him. He was an intimidating guy, it was part of his job, and yet she didn't even flinch or back down from his temper.

Just one more thing to like about her.

"What are you going to do about Beast?" Eve asked.

Oliver heard the concern in her tone, and his gaze shifted to the dog, who was lying on the floor of the kitchen with his face between his paws. Beast's eyes met his, and he lifted his head, panting. When Oliver didn't look away, the dog barked at him. His first instinct was to tell her the dog was going back, that he just didn't have the patience.

But then again, Eve liked Beast. He had noticed the way her face softened every time the dog nudged her for pets. And the sweet sound of her laughter at Beast's behavior was something he could listen to forever.

Shit, forever? What is happening to you?

Whatever it was, it had happened the minute Evelyn Reynolds walked into his life and threw him into chaos.

"I guess I'm gonna show him who's boss," Oliver said.

Eve's face lit up, and he knew he'd made the right choice. "Well, good luck with that," she said, chuckling. "I really don't think you scare him."

"Believe me, by the time I get through with him, he'll be a model dog."

Chapter Seven

"Son of a bitch, Best, you are supposed to be helping me, not getting your chuckles on." Oliver had been working with Best all morning, trying to get Beast to sit and stay, but the minute Oliver dropped the leash, Beast took off.

"Hey, it's not my fault he doesn't respect you," Best said. "Plus, you're a great example to the kids of what *not* to do."

Except for Jorge and Tommy, the group of eight teen-aged boys coughed, presumably to cover their laughter. But they would pay. They had been working in one of five fenced-in training yards, and all of the other dogs stood at their trainers' side, looking like model dogs.

"Hey, Sergeant Best, maybe you should take us back," Jorge said.

Oh, yes. Oliver would make them pay.

Oliver cursed as the damn dog went to Best, sitting on command.

"Well, how come he respects you?" Oliver grumbled.

"Because I respect him. Training dogs has as much to do with your attitude and behavior as it does theirs. He knows you don't respect him, and he's telling you that you should," Best said.

Oliver smacked Jorge upside the head as he went to retrieve the leash from Best.

"Yo, that's abuse!" Jorge said.

"Stop being a pussy," Darrel snapped.

Oliver grinned as Jorge spluttered. They had been training for eight days now, and Darrel had finally started to relax and come out of his shell. He also had a knack for putting the dogs at ease, talking to them in low tones. All the dogs responded to him, even Beast.

It was just Oliver who Beast still wasn't listening to.

At home, it was different. After their first night and day together, Oliver hadn't let Beast out of his sight. He took the big old dog everywhere with him, even in the shower. And though he'd never admit this to anyone, he had even given Beast a thorough scrub down with some dog shampoo he'd bought. Despite their current battle during training, Oliver had actually grown attached to the big mutt.

Now, if only Beast would follow one simple command.

At this point, Oliver was ready to give up, but Eve's smiling face crept into his mind each time he considered it. She'd called him every day, asking how his to-do list was going, but as professional as she tried to keep it, the conversation would eventually stray to training Beast. And when he'd say he just wasn't cut out for it, she'd tell him not to give up, that eventually Beast and he would find their rhythm.

Oliver wasn't as confident, but he wanted to make Eve happy.

"How do I show him that I respect him?"

Best pulled a bag of dog treats and a ball from his backpack and handed them to Oliver. "Positive reinforcement. Show him you like him and that you appreciate when he does something right."

Oliver put the bag in his pocket and held up the ball. "Okay, dude, I am at the end of my rope with you. You gotta meet me halfway, so if you want the ball, sit."

Beast's gaze shifted from him to the ball, and then he slowly sat.

"Good boy," Oliver said, keeping his voice low. "Here you go."

Oliver threw the ball, shocked at how fast Beast was. The brown blur of his body whizzed across the lawn and caught the ball in his mouth in seconds. He seemed to be contemplating whether or not to come back when Oliver called, "Come."

"Five to one he takes off running again," Tommy said. Oliver ignored him, refusing to break eye contact with Beast.

Beast tilted his head with the bright green ball hanging out the side of his mouth and finally started trotting back toward him.

When he stopped in front of Oliver and sat, Oliver hooked his leash on and took the ball from him. "Good dog."

Loud whoops and cheers emitted from the group of boys until Best yelled, "Knock it off!"

Beast's body shook, and Oliver could tell he was dying to run, but still he stayed seated. Oliver pulled a treat from his pocket and held it out for Beast, who took it gently from his palm. "Now, I'm going to put your leash down and I want you to stay."

Beast remained relaxed while Oliver set his leash on the ground. "Stay." Oliver stood up and took two steps away, surprised when Beast didn't move.

"Come."

Beast stood and lumbered over, plopping down at his feet expectantly.

This time, even Best applauded, and Oliver squatted down, taking Beast's head between his hands and rubbing his floppy ears. "Good boy."

"I was going to say the same thing to you."

Oliver looked over his shoulder to find Eve standing behind him, smiling. Her black hair was held away from her face with a headband and her black dress was a stark contrast to the paleness of her skin.

She looked fucking gorgeous.

"Damn," one of the boys said.

Oliver gave the group a hard stare, and Best shouted, "All right, turds, get your asses inside and put your dogs in their crates. I think you need a couple hours in the weight room."

Loud groans and curses rose up, but Best's scowl shut them up fast. Despite his easygoing nature, Best hadn't survived in the Marines because of his bad jokes.

When the kids were out of earshot, Oliver turned his attention back to Eve. "Hey, what are you doing here?"

"I just stopped by to see how the training was going," she said.

"We're getting better," Oliver said. He stood up, keeping a hold of Beast's leash so he didn't get drool on Eve's dress. "You look great. Hot date?"

He was surprised by how casual he sounded, even as he silently willed her to say no.

"Hardly. I'm heading up the hill with a few friends to go to Red Hawk Casino."

"I didn't take you for a gambler," Oliver teased, relieved.

"I'm not really, but I've never been, so it should be fun," she said. "What are you up to tonight?"

Oliver caught sight of Best by the fence, making a spanking motion with his hand. Oliver took a step toward him, but Eve turned around to see what had caught his attention and he blurted, "I'll probably just head out to Mick's with the guys."

"That sounds like fun," she said.

Heavy silence fell between them, and despite the tiny voice telling him not to ask, he couldn't help himself. "Did you really drive over here to check on training, or was there something else you wanted?"

A rosy hue spread over her cheeks, belying her words. "No, nothing else. I just wanted to make sure that everyone is going to be on their best behavior for the fund-raiser."

"I think we will be good," Oliver said.

He watched Eve, trying to read more into her words and expressions. After almost three weeks of talking and spending time with her, he still couldn't figure her out. Just when he started to think her resolve about being with him was softening, she'd put up that shield.

It had kept him in a perpetually frustrated state, and he hated it.

"Great," she said. "Well, I should probably go. I've got an hour drive up the hill, and I've got to pick up my friends, so…yeah."

"Got it, you got to go."

She shot him a glare, but he had no idea what he'd said to piss her off. He didn't even have a chance to ask before she was spinning on her heels and walking away.

What the hell was that about?

WHY AM I such an idiot?

It was the fiftieth time that night Eve had asked herself that, and still, an answer hadn't presented itself.

"Where are you, and why aren't you with your two besties having the time of your life?"

Eve turned to her friend Megan Bryce and answered her question with more snap than she intended. "Because the time of my life usually doesn't involve me losing money."

"Meow, what crawled up your butt?" Allison Breslin asked from the slot machine next to Megan.

"Yeah, you've been acting like a crankster since you picked us up," Megan said.

Eve sighed, feeling like a heel. "I'm sorry, guys, I'll shake it off."

"What's up?" Allison asked.

Eve considered telling her friends, but how could they really understand? Allison, also an army brat, was a sweet-faced blonde who had met her husband, Luke, while he'd been stationed in San Diego in the navy and she'd been at San Diego State. She understood Eve's point on marrying a military man, but she'd also told Eve that even if she lost her husband, she'd never regret the time she had with him.

And Megan, well, Megan had followed in her father and three older brothers' footsteps and joined the army right out of high school, eventually becoming an MP. She was tall, lean, and athletic with short brown hair and bright blue eyes. If she hadn't been injured and medically discharged, she would have been a lifer. The three of them had met in high school and clicked, staying close despite distance and hectic lives. Yet, when it came to what they wanted out of life, their ideals were very different.

"Nothing's up," Eve said. "I'll just be back to my normal, fun-loving self when this fund-raiser is over."

"Why, are the guys at the base giving you shit?" Megan asked.

"No, they're fine," Eve said.

"Evie, don't you know it's not nice to call people fucked up, insecure, neurotic, and emotional?" Megan joked. "Besides, I heard some women are into that sort of thing."

Eve looked at her slot machine, but she could feel Allison watching her.

"Do you like one of them?" Allison asked.

"Come on, Ali." Eve tried to sound derisive but didn't think it worked.

"Fuck me, you *do*!" Megan crowed.

"I don't!" Catching their skeptical looks, Eve reluctantly said, "Okay, I might, but I don't want to."

"Who is it? Come on, details, woman," Megan said.

"There are no details to tell. I don't even know if I like him, it's more that I just—"

"Want to strip him naked and eat chocolate off his abs?" Megan offered.

Eve thought about that, grinning. "His butt, too. He's got a great butt."

"So, do it. What's the hold up?" Allison asked.

"Well, my dad hates him, so that always makes things easy," Eve said.

"What did he do to piss off the general?" Megan asked, amused.

"Remember when I told you Hank got arrested a few weeks ago for drunk and disorderly conduct after fighting with a guy from the base?" Eve could tell they did because their eyes widened and they nodded. "Yep, I picked that guy. Out of all the guys I could fall for, I pick the one my brother and dad despise."

"Wait, *fall for*? Like, you could fall in love with this guy?" Allison asked.

"No, I mean…I just meant that I like him and I'm trying really hard not to. But then I find myself calling him for no reason and showing up at his work because I want to see him, only to make an ass out of myself…" Both of her friends were staring at her like she'd grown a third eye. She buried her face in her hands and groaned. "Ugh, what is wrong with me?"

"Could you be going through a late-in-life rebellion?" Eve shot Megan a glare, and she held her hands up. "Hey, the alternative is that you, Miss Evelyn Reynolds, are smitten with someone your father would definitely not approve of."

"Thanks for stating the obvious, Meg. How do I make it go away?" Eve asked.

"Why would you want it to?" Allison was watching her seriously, and Eve bit her lip to keep from saying the first thing she thought, which was that she didn't want her mother's life, but was that really how she felt? Her mother had been married to the same man for almost thirty years, had two grown, mostly well-adjusted children. There were worse things to aspire to.

"Because we aren't right for each other and I'm not looking for someone to just hang out and kill time with until I meet the right guy."

"Why aren't you right for each other?" Allison asked.

"You mean besides the obvious?" Eve thought for a moment. "He's never been in a relationship."

"Neither have you," Megan said.

"Yes, I have. I dated Dylan for almost six months."

"You only dated him that long because you were afraid to break up with him because he had stalker tendencies," Allison said.

"Fine, but I *would* have relationships if I found the right guy."

"Or maybe you're scared to find the right guy, so you self-sabotage," Allison said.

"How do I self-sabotage?"

"Your apartment, for one thing," Megan said.

"God, now you sound like my dad," Eve said.

"Look, we just think that maybe you're afraid of getting hurt, so you date guys you know will never measure up to your expectations and drive away the good ones," Allison said.

"Well, on that high note, I'm out of money," Eve said.

Megan stood up with her and wrapped her arms around Eve's stiff shoulders. "Come on, love, don't be pissy. We only say these things because we love you."

"Ha, I think you bear false love," Eve said, fighting a smile.

Allison hugged her, too, and before long, they were laughing. When they pulled away, Megan said, "Where is this bad boy who's got you wound up? Let's go check him out."

MICK'S BAR WAS in the heart of Old Town Sacramento, and the two-story building reminded Eve more of an old Western saloon than a dive bar. Eve had dropped Allison at home on the way down, but Megan had insisted on following her, wanting to get a look at "Mr. Chocolate Butt." As they wove through the crowd, Eve kept her eye out for Oliver.

"Holy yum, there is some talent here tonight!" Megan exclaimed.

Eve snagged a table in the corner, and as they sat down, she could have sworn she saw a familiar shaved head at the bar. She kept her eyes glued to the spot. A few bodies shifted, and there he was, leaning against the bar, smiling at a petite dark-haired girl in a short denim skirt.

Eve turned her face away, afraid he'd sense her gaze on him, and suddenly felt like a stalker. "This is stupid."

"Did you spot him?" Megan asked.

"Yeah, but he's busy." Eve didn't want to admit that the uncomfortable churning in her gut was jealousy, but she didn't like seeing him with another girl.

That smile was hers.

"Is he the stud in the blue shirt talking to the tiny cheerleader?" Megan asked. At Eve's nod, Megan whistled. "Nice. He definitely looks edible."

"Dude, stop staring or he's going to see you," Eve warned.

"Too late," Megan said. "He's coming over."

"What?" Eve turned in her seat, and sure enough, Oliver was heading their way with a gigantic grin on his face. Her heart did a little leap of joy as she noted that he'd ditched his companion the minute he'd spotted her.

"Hey, what are you doing here?" he asked. One of his hands rested on the back of her chair, and the brush of his hand against the bare skin of her shoulder sent shivers down her spine.

"Just felt like getting a drink. Oliver, this is my friend Megan."

"Hey, Megan," Oliver said. He leaned over Eve's shoulder to hold out his hand to Megan. As he did so, he pressed against Eve, and it affected her—like pulse-racing, skin-on-fire, drumming-tempo-between-her-thighs affected her.

"Oliver, so nice to meet you. Eve just keeps going on and on about your b—"

Eve kicked Megan hard in the shin and glared at her furiously.

"You've been talking about me, huh?" Oliver asked. Eve glanced at him and caught his satisfied smile.

"I was just telling her about us working together," she said.

"Of course, that's what I thought she meant. Why else would you be talking about me?"

Megan laughed at his teasing, and Eve silently vowed revenge.

"Can I get you ladies a drink? You are more than welcome to join me and the guys downstairs," Oliver said.

"Actually, I just remembered that I have to be up early tomorrow," Megan said, hopping out of her chair.

Eve stared hard at Megan and mouthed *I'm going to kill you.* Megan mouthed back *you'll thank me.*

"Well, that's too bad, maybe next time," Oliver said.

"Definitely." Megan gave her a little finger wave and took off, leaving Eve alone with Oliver.

"She set you up good, huh?"

Eve turned in her seat and smiled sheepishly. "Yes, she did."

Oliver slid a piece of hair that had escaped from her headband behind her ear. "I'm glad you came."

"I'm not crashing your party?" Eve hated asking, but the woman at the bar still bothered her.

The meaning behind her words seemed to dawn on him, and he shook his head. "There was never going to be a party. The plan was to stay a couple hours and go home to let Beast out of his kennel." Then he went and shattered her, leaning over to whisper in her ear, "And then I was going to lie down and think of you until I fell asleep."

His words were heady, and before she could think of the repercussions, she grabbed him by the back of the head and pulled him down for a kiss.

OLIVER MET EVE'S lips and took charge, stepping into her sitting form and sliding his tongue inside her open mouth. From the minute he'd seen Megan staring at him and recognized the back of Eve's head, he'd hoped she was there for him. He wasn't a romantic guy, at least, he never used to be, but Eve made him say things—feel things—he wasn't sure what to make of, and at times, they made him want to run the other way.

But right now, he didn't want to run. He wasn't thinking of his career, his friends waiting for him downstairs, or even Evelyn's dad. His mind, body, and senses were so filled with her that there wasn't room for anything else. The noise from the bar faded to a dull roar as she gripped his shirt and pulled him as close as he could get and his hands settled on her hips.

Suddenly, a voice Oliver recognized broke through the hum. "Ow, Martinez, you are getting me hot, bro!"

Oliver pulled away and whispered, "I am so sorry."

"Why?" she asked.

Oliver turned, keeping Eve behind him. "What's up, Tate?"

Kevin Tate was an MP, and although Oliver worked with him, he didn't like the obnoxious asshole. Oliver saw that most of his squad was with Tate and nodded at them.

"Nothing, just getting some beers with the guys," Tate said, trying to look around Oliver. "Who's your friend?"

"None of your business," Oliver said. He was pissed at Tate for interrupting but more concerned with Tate knowing who Evelyn was. Everyone knew about the beef between the general and him, and he wouldn't put it past Tate to think that Oliver was using Eve to get back at her old man.

And Oliver was scared as hell she might believe it.

"What's the matter, Martinez, she ugly or something?" This came from Dwight Cameron, whose glassy-eyed expression said he'd had one too many already.

"Oh, jeez, this is ridiculous," Eve said at his back. He felt her push at him so she could stand and come around to his side. "Satisfied, gentleman?"

The group of men stared at her, some in appreciation, but a few in surprised recognition.

"Eve?" a guy Oliver didn't recognize said. He was medium height with blue eyes and sandy blond hair.

Eve looked unhappy to see him. "Andy."

"It's been a long time," he said.

"Not nearly long enough."

The guys snickered and coughed, and Andy's cheeks flushed angrily. "I see you still got a thing for guys in uniform."

Oliver didn't like the guy's insinuation that Eve was a uniform chaser and barely resisted the urge to pop him.

"Actually, I don't," she said.

A twinge of disappointment pinched Oliver's chest, but to his surprise, she took his hand. "But I'm making an exception for this guy."

Andy's smirk melted away.

"Wanna get out of here?" she asked, her tone flirty and seductive.

Oliver squeezed her hand. "Lead the way."

Chapter Eight

EVE'S HEAD SPUN as they walked along the rows of old buildings, neither of them speaking. Part of her had been humiliated when Andy had alluded to her infatuation with him, and she'd wanted to tuck tail and run, to get far away from all of them and never look back.

But then she'd seen Oliver's face. He'd been staring at Andy as if he'd wanted to separate Andy's head from his shoulders, and she realized it was because he cared about her. He'd been ready to protect her, and suddenly, she hadn't cared what Andy or his goons thought of her.

All that mattered was how she felt about Oliver.

"So, you and that guy…"

Oliver's unfinished question was hesitant, as if he was afraid to ask, and she smiled. "We snuck around one summer, before I found out it was some kind of challenge his bunkmates and he came up with. Part of the reason I avoid military guys as a rule. They either want me because they want to get at my dad or to prove something to their friends."

Oliver stopped and pulled her into him, leaning against the front of a darkened clothing store. "You know that this thing between us has nothing to do with your father, don't you?"

"I wouldn't be here if I thought that."

Oliver cupped her face and brushed her lips gently with his, liquefying her insides and setting her knees to melt-down mode. She gripped his arms as he deepened the kiss, coaxing her sweetly to rest her body against his. His hands moved down to encircle her waist, his big palms resting on her lower back, just above her butt.

Pulling her mouth away from his, she gasped, "Maybe we should take this someplace a little less public? After all, we haven't exactly had the best of luck making out in plain sight."

"Oh. God, yes," he groaned. Taking her hand, he strode down the sidewalk, dragging her along with him.

Eve laughed, thrilled he was as caught up in her as she was in him. "Let's go back to your place."

"I wanna see yours," he said.

Nope, bad idea. Not only was her apartment looking a little worse for the wear, again, but it would be just her luck if her dad showed up while Oliver was there.

"But you said that you had to let Beast out," she said.

"Well, I'll go let him out and meet you back at yours."

"There's no point in you going home, just to drive back out again," she said.

Oliver stopped, staring down at her with suspicion lurking in his eyes. "Are you a hoarder or something?"

"What? No."

"Then why don't you want me to come over?" he asked.

"Because I haven't had a chance to pick up and there could be things I don't want you to see."

"Like?"

"I don't know, dishes in the sink? Bras hanging over doorknobs? It just isn't company-ready," she said. His persistence, while usually endearing when it was in the pursuit of her, was irritating now.

Suddenly, he swung her up in his arms and gave her a smacking kiss to cover her squeal. "Fine, I'll give you some notice before I invite myself over. But for the record, you can leave the bras anywhere you want."

Her good mood restored, she wrapped her arms around his shoulders and raised her eyebrow. "You're kind of a pervert, aren't you? I bet you go through panty drawers, too."

"Is that an invitation?" he asked.

"As long as you don't try any of them on, I'm okay with it," she said. His startled expression set her off into peals of laughter. When he set her on her feet, she had to lean against him she was so overcome with mirth.

"For the record, I have never worn women's underwear."

"Just one more thing I like about you," she said breathlessly.

"So, wait, are you saying you like-like me?" he teased.

"No, but I'm toying with the idea," she said.

"Why you gotta be so cold?" he asked.

Raising herself on tiptoe, she gave him a kiss so heated the air around them turned humid. "Take me back to your place, and I'll show you how hot I can be."

OLIVER PULLED INTO his driveway and practically jumped out of the car. He had probably broken the speed limit and performed several California rolls, but he'd wanted to let Beast outside and get him all squared away before Eve got there.

Seeing her headlights in the distance, he rushed inside, but as soon as he stepped through the door he knew something was wrong. The metallic smell of blood was strong, and as he came around the side of the couch and flipped on the light, he saw the mangled bars of the cage where it looked like Beast had bitten through the metal. Only he hadn't chewed the hole big enough, and his large head and neck were stuck. His flat, brown muzzle was covered in blood, and he whimpered softly, hardly moving.

"Fuck," Oliver said. He knelt on the floor, and blood seeped into his pants as he studied the way the metal had scraped and gouged into Beast's skin, cutting into the muscle. It looked as if he'd been struggling for hours, and his movements had just further embedded the sharp, broken metal.

"Okay, buddy, I know it hurts, but you need to stay still, okay? I'm going to get something to cut the wire."

"Oh, God," Eve said behind him.

He hadn't even heard her come in, but as he stood up, he whispered, "Keep him calm, and don't let him move.

Those wounds in his neck are deep, and I don't want him puncturing anything."

Eve nodded and knelt down in his place, talking softly to Beast. Oliver ran through the house to the garage, raiding his tool box for wire cutters. When he found what he needed, he grabbed a bunch of rags and headed back inside.

He settled next to Eve and realized his hands were shaking as he started cutting the wires around Beast's neck. Every time the dog whimpered, he winced and tried to calmly reassure him. He heard Eve's sniffles and knew she was crying, but he couldn't comfort her now. All he could think about was getting his dog help.

Fifteen minutes later, he cut through the last wires and was able to move Beast's head back into the cage while Eve opened the front of it so he could step out. Blood oozed from the raw, pink wounds, and Oliver didn't hesitate before picking Beast up in his arms.

"Can you look up the nearest twenty-four-hour veterinarian?" He didn't like the way Beast's head and neck seemed to be swelling.

"There's one on Watt Avenue I've taken Matilda to," Eve said. "I know how to get there. You hold him, I'll drive."

Oliver didn't argue, just followed her outside, climbed into her passenger seat, and settled Beast on his lap. He realized that as much as he'd resisted bonding with Beast, it had happened anyway. Despite how crazy Beast made him, he'd come to love the big, stupid mutt.

Once Eve pulled into the veterinarian's parking lot, Oliver could hardly wait for her to get the door for him. They entered the office, and Eve called out, "Can someone please help us?"

A stocky woman with short brown hair came around the desk. "What happened here?"

"I left him alone in his metal kennel, and he chewed through the bars. I came home, and his head was stuck, there was blood all over his face and neck. I cut the cage off him, but his neck and head seem to be swelling, and there are these deep gouges—"

"How long was he alone for?" she asked.

"About three hours."

"Let's carry him into the back. Is there anything wrong with his limbs?"

"No, I just didn't want to put a leash on him," Oliver said.

"Well, let's get a look at him."

They followed her through the door, and she pointed toward a stainless steel table. The sound of yipping dogs agitated Beast, and he started to struggle against Oliver. Eve reached out and touched Beast's head, whispering to him. Oliver set him down on the table gently, keeping a hand on him and stroking his back.

"Hang on, dude. I know it's scary, but we're gonna make you feel better," the technician said kindly. Oliver caught sight of her name tag. *Karen.* "Is he allergic to any medications?"

"I don't know," Oliver said.

"How about a history of separation anxiety?" she asked.

"I've had him less than two weeks and haven't really left him alone. At least, not since he destroyed my couch the day I brought him home," he said.

"Well, it definitely sounds like the big guy does not like to be separated from his person. We're going to give him a sedative and let our vet get a better look at these wounds to make sure there are no punctures or other concerns." Her matter-of-fact confidence reassured Oliver. "Hey, Josie, can you help me get…What's his name?" Karen asked Oliver.

"Beast."

The tech grinned. "Like from *The Sandlot*? It's fitting. He looks like he might have some mastiff in him."

Josie, another technician, came over and laid a calming hand on the dog's back. "Shh, it's okay, big guy."

Oliver and Eve stepped back, and Beast started twisting to sit up.

"Hang on, Dad and Mom, we're gonna need you to stand up by his head and talk to him while we get his weight and prepare his drugs." Karen disappeared, and Eve rubbed her hand over Oliver's back as he stepped around Josie, kneeling so he was eye to eye with Beast.

"Hey, dude. Look, I'm sorry I didn't figure out that you really couldn't be left alone. I feel like a tool, but I promise, if you come out of this I'll share my eggs with you every morning for a week."

He heard a wet laugh behind him and looked up at Eve, who was brushing at her eyes rapidly.

Beast whined, and his big, pink tongue snaked out, catching Oliver right on the nose, but he didn't care.

Karen came back and drew up some clear liquid in a syringe. "All right, buddy, now this might sting a bit, but Dad's right here and he's going to talk you through it. Josie is just going to keep you still."

Beast hardly flinched as she administered the sedative, and within moments, his whole body relaxed.

"If you want to go to the front desk and fill out a new client form, we'll call you with an update as soon as the doc finishes," Karen said.

"Can't I just wait in the lobby?" Oliver asked.

"You can, but it might be awhile, especially since Beast will be a little groggy from the anesthetic. I promise, as soon as he starts waking up, I'll give you a buzz and you can rush back over."

Oliver didn't argue, and with one last stroke of Beast's big head, he walked through the doors to the lobby. Eve caught up to him and slipped her hand in his, giving it a squeeze.

Thirty minutes later, they arrived back at his place, and he was surprised when she asked to come in.

"I figure I can help clean up the cage, and the floor, and, well, you."

Oliver looked down at his shirt and pants, which were covered in blood, and nodded. "Thanks, I'd appreciate it."

He opened the door and let her in first, hardly knowing what to say. Guilt swirled inside Oliver, berating him for not having realized that there was something more going on with Beast than simply adjusting to a new environment. There was something Oliver could or should have done, and it pissed him off that he had gone to the bar tonight. He should have been home with Beast.

"This wasn't your fault," Eve said, practically reading his mind.

"Well, it's somebody's fault, so it might as well be mine."

"Have you ever had a dog? Not just when you were a kid, but one that you were solely responsible for?"

"No," he said.

"Then how were you supposed to know what to look for, let alone realize that Beast had a serious disorder? I mean, dogs chew things when they're bored. It was a simple mistake," she said.

"But if Best had entrusted Beast to someone with more experience, they might have caught his issues and…"

"And what? Sent him back to the shelter? You actually think he'd be better off there than with someone who cares about him?" Eve said.

"I just think that he deserves more than I can give him," Oliver said. Picking up Beast's cage, he carried it outside and set it in the backyard. Tomorrow he'd take it to the dump, but for right now, he just needed it out of his sight.

When he came back through the door, Eve was rummaging through his cupboards.

"What are you looking for?" he asked.

"A bucket and floor cleaner, so I can mop up the… blood," she said.

"There's no bucket, but the cleaning supplies are under the sink," he said.

Eve bent out of sight and popped back up with a bottle in her hand. She set it on the counter and walked over to him, wrapping her arms around his waist.

"Look, I know tonight was scary, but I've seen you with him. I've heard the way you talk about him. You love him. That's all he needs. He's not going to get better than that, anywhere."

Oliver wished he could agree with her, but he was completely out of his depth here.

"The dog's not really mine anyway," Oliver said. "I'm supposed to be training him to be a military dog, which means he'll go from me to someone else, but after this, Best probably will need to replace him."

Eve tipped her face up. "So adopt him."

"If he's not in the program, I highly doubt Best is going to let me cart him back and forth to the facility, and besides, what happens when I go back to full MP duty?" Oliver shook his head, wondering how he'd never thought of this before. "This was supposed to be a temporary thing."

Eve pulled away, and Oliver could sense her hurt even without words.

"What did I say?" he asked.

Eve didn't answer. Frustrated, Oliver took her shoulders in his hands and turned her to face him again, but she avoided his gaze. "Hey, answer me."

But still she said nothing, and he felt his frayed nerves unraveling.

"Eve, what in the hell is the matter with you? I am in no mood to play games right now."

"Okay, fine," she said, her green eyes blazing up at him finally. "When you were talking about this only being temporary, did you mean the job, Beast, or—by extension—were you talking about me?"

"Of course I wasn't talking about you," he snapped.

"So, it was the job, then," she said. "When you get back to your real job, what hours do you usually work?"

Oliver didn't like where this was going but he wasn't going to avoid it, either. "The night shift, but depending on what we're working on, the hours can be longer."

"And is your job dangerous?"

It was a trick question, and he knew any way he answered it, he was screwed. "I'm a police officer on a military base where everyone has a gun. Depending on the call, yeah, my job can be dangerous."

"And what about being deployed? Could that happen?"

"You know it could." Oliver softened his voice and ran his hands over her shoulders, willing her to understand and accept him. All of him. "You grew up with a dad in the military. You know I can get a new post at any time; if there's a war, I can be deployed, and yes, if I take the wrong call on the wrong night, I could be dealing with a scary situation, but that's not going to stop me from doing my job, Eve. I'm good at it."

"I know," Eve said. "I knew that before you said the words, but I ignored it for a little while because despite my better judgment, I do like you. But it isn't just one bad experience that has kept me from dating guys like you. I want a guy who is safe, who is going to be home with me at night to eat dinner and watch TV. I don't want to get involved with a guy I might not see for years on end or who might not come home because he has to deal with dangerous situations all day. For a moment there, I thought I could put all those things aside because I liked you, but I still want a normal, safe life."

Oliver released her shoulders, squeezing his hands into tight fists at his side. "A normal, safe guy could die in a car crash."

"That would be horribly tragic, but he wouldn't be putting himself in harm's way daily or be separated from me. I'm afraid that if I keep letting myself get close to you, I'm going to forget that I don't want these things because I'll want you more."

Hope swept through Oliver at her words, and he wished he knew the right thing to make her understand that this was who he was. He helped people, and there was nothing wrong with that. He could still have it all; they could still spend time together. Their schedules just might be a little different than those of other couples.

"Come on, Eve, we've had a rough night—"

"And after one rough night you give up on Beast without even putting up a fight. Kinda says a lot about how much you value your relationships," she said.

That glimmer of hope was snuffed out by a blaze of fury that tightened every muscle in his body and burned across his skin.

"Are you actually comparing the way I feel about you to my connection with a dog?"

"No, God, I don't know. Okay?" With a heavy sigh, she pushed past him toward the door, but he was too exhausted to follow.

Chapter Nine

OLIVER STOOD IN Sparks's office the next morning, spoiling for a fight. Between worrying about Beast and being frustrated by Eve's attitude, he'd hardly slept at all last night. Most women would've been wetting themselves, calling him a hero, but he'd managed to fall for the one woman who actually looked at his dedication to his job and country as a drawback. And now, he had to fight to keep Beast.

"I don't give a fuck what you think, he's not going back to the shelter," Oliver said roughly.

"I didn't say he had to go back to the shelter," Sparks said.

"But he can't be in the program," Best added, earning a threatening look from Oliver. Best threw his hands up in a don't-shoot-the-messenger gesture. "I'm just saying that these dogs go through so much, it wouldn't work for him. It doesn't mean we can't find him a good home."

"As long as I can bring him to work with me, I'd like to keep him," Oliver said.

"What happens when you get put back on patrol?" Sparks asked.

"That's another thing I'd like to discuss. If you have somewhere you can use me, mentoring, or running social media, or hell, scooping dog shit, I'm in." He could tell he'd surprised Sparks and Best, but the idea had been rolling around in his mind all night. He could provide a home for Beast. Besides, he actually enjoyed working with the kids, and although he had never considered himself the mentoring type, he'd enjoyed spending time with Tommy, Darrel, and Jorge.

Even if he wasn't upholding the law, he was helping people. That was all he'd ever wanted to do.

And maybe Eve would consider being with you if your job was less dangerous?

Oliver told himself his decision had nothing to do with her, but it definitely felt like a lie. The truth was, while he'd been lying awake last night, he'd pictured his future. He hadn't been surrounded by medals and trophies. He'd been sitting in the living room of his house, watching TV, and then suddenly, a woman sat down in his lap and handed him a beer.

That woman had been Eve.

Best and Sparks exchanged heavy glances, and Oliver gritted his teeth. "What? You think I'm a bad fit?"

"No, but we just want to make sure this is really what you want," Sparks said.

"Yeah, it is."

"Then I hope you don't mind working with the MP and police dogs we're training," Best said. "I'll go order one of those full-body attack training suits for you." Best clapped him on the back on his way out of Sparks's office.

Oliver kicked out at Best as he left, but Best dodged his boot with a laugh.

And then it was just him and Sparks.

"You know you're going to have to talk with General Reynolds about making your position permanent."

"Yeah, I know," Oliver said grimly. "That's my next stop. I made an appointment at eleven."

Dean raised his eyebrows. "You were that sure we were going to want to stare at your ugly mug every day?"

"I was banking on it," Oliver said.

EVE'S HEAD WAS hammering. Whether it was from the total lack of sleep or the half a bottle of wine she'd downed when she'd gotten home, she wasn't sure. Even Matilda's cries to be fed were earsplitting, and Eve covered her head with a pillow to block out the noise.

Suddenly, she felt Matilda jump up onto the bed and step on her legs before sitting on the small of Eve's back. Tiny, bony paws kneaded her back, and Eve winced as Matilda's sharp claws broke through her T-shirt, scraping her skin.

"Okay, ow, I'm up," Eve said, squirming. Matilda jumped off her back, and when Eve turned onto her side and lifted the pillow, Matilda was staring back at her with a bored expression on the white mask of her face, her tail twitching back and forth like a black snake.

"You are a mean cat. I scoop your poop, give you fresh water, and feed you more than I should, and you can't let me sleep ten extra minutes?"

"*Rouw,*" Matilda answered.

"I guess that's a no," Eve said. She sat up slowly, clutching her head with one hand and groaning. "No more wine, ever."

Grabbing her glasses off of her nightstand, she finally got to her feet and padded to the bathroom, unpleasant flashes of last night assaulted her. The most haunting of which was the expression on Oliver's face when she'd basically told him that she didn't want him. For such a big, hard guy, he'd looked so sad, so lost. She'd sat in her car for a while, debating whether she should get out and apologize or get the hell out of there. In the end, she'd driven home and regretted every mile, every minute that put distance between her and Oliver.

But what was she supposed to do? Put aside her principles because she liked him? What happened when it all went to hell and she was looking back, thinking to herself, *I knew I shouldn't have done that?*

The shrill blare of "Mamma Mia" exploded from her bedroom, and she stumbled out of the bathroom to answer her cell.

"Hey, Mom," she said.

"Hello, Sweetie, you sound terrible. Are you sick?" her mother asked.

"Nope, just hungover," Eve said.

"Oh, well in that case, take a shower and come meet me for lunch."

The thought of food sent her stomach into a churning ball of protest. "I'm not really hungry."

"You will be, and besides, we haven't had a mother-daughter day in a while, and I want a chance to catch up. It's hard being an empty nester."

The guilt trip worked like a charm. "Okay, where do you want to meet?"

OLIVER SAT IN the general's office, admiring his framed metals and pictures, but there was one on his desk that made him sit forward. Picking up the old wooden frame, Oliver smiled at a younger version of the general dancing with a little girl with black curls and a red flowing dress.

"Have you ever heard the phrase 'look but don't touch'?" a deep voice said behind him.

Oliver set the picture back on the general's desk and stood up, saluting him. "I apologize, sir."

"At ease." General Reynolds was in good physical shape for his age, and despite being several inches shorter than Oliver, he was still an imposing figure. The general sat down and waved his hand to the chair behind Oliver, indicating he should sit, too. "What is it I can do for you, Sergeant Martinez?"

Oliver sat and ran his hands over his legs nervously, wiping his sweaty palms on his pants. "I wanted to talk to you about staying on at Alpha Dog, sir. I've enjoyed my time there and would like to continue, instead of returning to my unit."

"I see," the general said. "And have you also enjoyed working with my daughter, Sergeant Martinez?"

What does Eve have to do with this? Oliver didn't know what Eve had told him, but he treaded lightly. "I have, sir. She is a wonderful woman, and you should be proud of her, but she has nothing to do with my decision to stay on. I enjoy working with the kids and the dogs and feel like I can make a difference there. And they have a spot for me."

"You say that she has nothing to do with your decision to stay on, but I find that hard to believe. Don't think I haven't noticed the way she talks about you."

She talks about me with her family? Oliver smothered his excitement as the general added, "And I am proud of her, most definitely. I am also very protective of her and do not want to see her hurt."

"That's the last thing I want as well, sir."

"Then you understand why I'm denying your request and transferring you back to active MP rotation first thing Tuesday morning. That should give you a long weekend to readjust."

The general's blunt announcement took him completely by surprise. "Sir, do you really think that putting me back in rotation will keep me away from her?"

"I know my daughter, Sergeant Martinez. Right now, you're accessible, but that will change," the general said. "Evelyn has never been shy about her opinions and desires for what she wants out of life, and I can guarantee you that you are not her future."

"You don't know that," Oliver said, forgetting himself and who he was talking to.

The general ignored his outburst, though. "It's my fault, really. I let my emotions get the better of me and wanted to teach you a lesson. Instead, I put my daughter in a position of vulnerability, and you took full advantage. I am willing to overlook your infraction and put you back where you belong, no harm, no foul."

"I never took advantage of Evelyn. What is between us has nothing to do with you and everything to do with her amazing spirit. I'm not giving up on her."

"Son, my daughter has plans for her life that do not include you. Whatever you think you feel for Eve, if you really cared, you'd let her go." The general's tone wasn't condescending or hostile; in fact, he sounded a little sad. "Men like you and I live our jobs. If I give you this position, you might be satisfied for a month or so, but then you're going to get antsy, and the urge for more is going to get stronger. You want to climb the ladder—I've read your file—and that requires long hours and a lot of sacrifice. And I don't want that for my daughter."

"You know her," Oliver said. "How could you put us together and never imagine I would fall for her?"

Oliver couldn't even believe he was saying this, but he felt every word in his gut and knew it was true. He was willing to fight for Eve. She was worth it.

"Honestly?" A sheepish grin broke under the general's salt and pepper mustache. "I thought she'd run you off the first day."

"She tried, but I'm stubborn. I don't give up easily, and if I have to, I can go over your head, sir," Oliver said.

His words wiped the smile from the general's face. "And I could have you transferred to another base, and then this conversation would be moot." The general stood up and said, "I'm giving you an out, Sergeant Martinez. I expect you to take it. Now, if you'll excuse me, I need to be somewhere."

The dismissive certainty in the general's order filled Oliver with impotent rage, as if it had never crossed the general's mind that Oliver would really go against him. Oliver exited the office, frustration vibrating through his muscles.

But it wasn't just that the general didn't believe that he'd fight for Eve. What if he was right that Oliver would just end up as one of Eve's regrets?

Damn it, he wasn't this guy, ruled by what-ifs and insecurities. He jumped in and went after what he wanted, yet here he was, debating and hee-hawing like an asshole.

He wanted to punch something, bust his fist through something hard and fleshy.

As he crossed the base back to his car, Tate and Andy, the man who had hurt Eve all those years ago, were coming out of one of the buildings. Tate waved, and although Oliver tried to ignore them, they intercepted him.

"Hey, Martinez, when you coming back for good?" Tate asked.

"Next week, apparently."

"That's great!" Tate slapped Oliver on the shoulder and lowered his voice, "Hey, man, I gotta ask…What was it like to do Reynolds's daughter? Because Andy here, he never got farther than second base, and I'm just thinking—"

Oliver didn't even remember attacking Tate. It was like a cloud of black and red swirled around him as he took the other man to the ground and threw a fist that shattered the bones and tissue under his knuckles. Oliver was oblivious to Tate's groan and the sound of gurgling, even Andy's faint shouts and arms grabbing at him, trying to drag him off. Oliver reached behind him, catching Andy was by the waist, and tossed him over his shoulder.

Finally, Oliver was slammed to the ground, pinned by Andy's heavy weight. As Andy jerked his arms behind his back, he felt a flash of stinging pain and realized Tate was kicking him in the ribs. The cloud evaporated, and Oliver grunted as another kick caught him in the midsection before he was pulled to his feet.

"Stupid asshole." Tate spat at him, his face covered in blood and his nose bent and swollen. "You are fucking screwed."

Just as Tate looked like he was going to make a move again, Andy snapped, "Just leave it, Tate. The last thing we need is the general getting involved and asking questions. Something tells me Oliver here won't mind repeating everything you said about his darling Eve."

Oliver glowered at Tate as he wiped off his face and gave Oliver a feral smile. "Man, Martinez, if she's that good of a piece of ass, I might just try her out myself."

"You're not her type, Tate. She doesn't go for pussies."

Tate's fist swung, and Oliver heard a cracking sound as it met his cheek. And then everything went black.

EVE SAT ACROSS from her mother, squinting her eyes at the menu. "Did we have to sit outside? The sun is hurting my eyes."

Her mother looked up from stirring her coffee, her green eyes worried. Eve had inherited her eyes, nose, and mouth, but the rest of her genetic makeup came from her father's side of the family. She wished sometimes that she'd been more of the natural beauty her mother was, but life was too short for comparisons. She did hope she got her mother's youthful skin as she aged. Although she was in her late fifties, her mother looked much younger.

"You poor baby, did you take any Tylenol? I don't know how many times I've warned you about having more than one glass of wine before bed."

Eve shot her mother a glare. "Sympathy *and* an I-told-you-so in one sentence? Congratulations, Mom, your attempt to make me feel better has failed."

"Are you going to tell me what brought on this late-night bender?"

Eve debated on confiding in her about Oliver, but considering her mother had been the one to sway her away from military men in the first place, Eve doubted she would feel much sympathy.

"I just had a rough couple of weeks, that's all," she said.

"Is it this charity event your father asked you to organize? I told him that you're serious about this PR company and don't need the extra stress of pro bono work when you're just starting out. Really, you should be getting paid for everything you're doing for them."

"No, it's been fine and a great way to get my name out there. I just…"

Ah, to hell with it. She needed to talk to someone. "Mom, I know you didn't want me joining or marrying into the military, but have you honestly ever regretted marrying Dad?"

Her mother paused with the coffee cup at her lips, then took a sip, as if considering what she was going to say. "No, Evie, I've never regretted marrying your father or the life we built. And it's not that I don't want you marrying into the military, that's more your father. I just saw the way that boy hurt you, and I honestly thought you were too young to get serious with anyone. Especially men in the military, who grow up fast and hard." She set her coffee down and asked, "Is there someone in particular you're interested in?"

"Yes, but I'm pretty sure I blew it by telling him I don't go for guys in uniform," she said.

"Who is he? Do I know him?"

Eve hesitated. "Not…really." When her mother raised her eyebrows expectantly, Eve sighed. "His name is Oliver Martinez. He's been working on the charity event with me."

"Martinez. Why do I know that name?"

"He was the soldier who got into a fight with Hank the night he was arrested," Eve offered.

"Oh, dear." Her mother covered her mouth, and Eve thought it was in horror at first, but then she heard a snort escape.

"Are you laughing?"

Her mother exploded into a fit of giggles, wiping at her eyes when they teared. "Of course you would be interested in the one man your father and brother despise."

"To be fair, Oliver said Hank was drunk and getting handsy with some girls. When Oliver told him to stop, Hank threw the first punch."

"And that may be so, but it doesn't change the fact that you two are going to have a battle on your hands with your father," her mother said.

"But not with you?" Eve asked.

"Not as long as he's good to you."

"I think he would be, but it's hard to tell since we've never really gotten that far. I mean, we've hung out and kissed, but it hasn't exactly been a normal courtship."

Her mother patted her hand and smiled. "Normal is boring. At least now you'll have a real story to tell my future grandchildren."

"Let's not get ahead of ourselves, Mother. I'd like to get through at least one date with the man before you have me barefoot and pregnant."

Chapter Ten

ON THE DAY of the charity event, everything was running smoothly as Eve left the gym where the educational demonstrations would be held. The military and police dog trainers would be up first to explain the process of training the dogs and even do a takedown demonstration. After they finished, search and rescue would do a mock rescue. There would be an hour-long break for lunch, and then the therapy dogs would complete the demonstrations.

The Rio Linda High School campus had turned out to be the perfect venue for the event. All the vendors were in place in the football field, wristbands were being purchased in the Quad, and she'd hired extra security, just in case. The dogs in training were all wearing their new Alpha Dog outfits, and they looked even better than Eve had hoped. The number of people who had turned out already was incredible.

The auditorium was being readied for the auction, and the adoptable dogs were being groomed just behind the large building. It was all going according to plan.

But there was one thing missing, and it had Eve ready to pull her hair out.

Oliver.

She hadn't seen or heard from him in two days, and she was worried. She'd even called his cell phone, but it had gone straight to voicemail.

Eve caught sight of Best working with one of the dogs outside the gym and asked, "Have you seen Oliver? I can't find him anywhere."

"Yeah, I saw him a few minutes ago," Best said. "I think he was taking Beast over to get fitted for an Alpha Dog shirt."

"Thanks." She headed toward the open classroom the school had offered for them to store things. She hated that Oliver was avoiding her, but she couldn't really blame him after what she'd said at his place. She needed to apologize and make things right with him.

But she had to find him first.

"Hey, Eve, we got a problem!" someone called out.

Ah, hell, and everything was going so well.

Eve turned, pushing up her glasses as they slid down her nose, and found Sergeant Sparks coming toward her. "What's up?"

"One of our trainers was involved in a car accident and can't make it," he said grimly.

"Which one?" she asked. "Are they okay?"

"It's Rivers, and yeah, she's okay, but her car is mangled."

Double shit. Rivers was an attractive blonde woman scheduled to lead out the third dog during the auction.

"Okay, we just need someone to fill in. Someone who has experience with dogs…" She racked her brain, willing herself not to panic.

"Maybe we can just have one of the trainers double up with a second dog," Sergeant Sparks suggested.

Eve hated that idea but didn't say it. They could probably scrounge up another male trainer, but there were so few female members of the Alpha Dog program…

"Megan!" Eve hadn't meant to shout, but she was just too excited. She'd asked Megan to come along and help, so she was here somewhere. She had MP training and had done guide-dog training in 4H.

"Megan who?" Sparks asked.

"Never mind, I've got it covered." Oliver would have to wait a minute or two until she talked to Megan.

Near the vendor tents, she found Megan grabbing a deep-fried Twinkie.

"I need you," Eve said, panting.

"Aw, I know. That's why I stick around," Megan said.

"I need you to stand in for a trainer who can't be here," Eve said.

"Ha-ha, you're funny," she said.

"Come on, you have the experience. You can smile, charm them, and show a couple basic behavior tips. Just go home and get your uniform."

"Girl, I am not—"

"Do you remember the time that I picked you up from that bar in Bakersfield you weren't supposed to be at when your car wouldn't start and you didn't want to call your parents?" Eve asked.

"Oh come on, that was nine years ago!" Megan said.

"And it's time to pay the piper, baby," Eve said.

Megan bit into her Twinkie aggressively and mumbled, "You are an evil wench."

"Yes, and you love me for it. Now hurry up! I need you back here in"—Eve checked her phone—"an hour and a half."

Megan threw her container away and stomped off, but Eve wasn't worried about her friend staying mad at her.

And now, to find Oliver.

"WILL YOU HOLD still?" Oliver griped at Beast, who looked a lot like the dog version of Frankenstein. The veterinarian had stitched up several large lacerations on his head and neck, but the shaved skin and wounds still looked gnarly. Oliver had picked up a doggie turtleneck at PetSmart per the vet's suggestion as an extra barrier in case he tried to scratch at the stitches on his neck. The trouble was getting it on Beast, who, after two days of pain meds and antibiotics in hotdogs, had become a spoiled brat. And he hated the shirt.

"Dude, at least its green camo. I could have gotten the pink one, so count your blessings," Oliver said. They had just picked up Beast's Alpha Dog jacket, but the turtleneck had to go on first or he was afraid the strap would irritate Beast's neck.

Since Oliver couldn't leave Beast on his own, he'd been switched from the auction to selling raffle tickets.

It wasn't such a bad deal, especially since it gave Beast a job, and he wouldn't have to spend an hour trying to make small talk with a stranger on how to make a dog sit. Wandering around the event also gave him the best opportunity to take pictures and videos to share online, since according to the very curt text message from Eve, he was still her right-hand man.

At least the job would keep him from obsessing over wanting more.

Finally getting the shirt over the dog's head, he lifted one paw and then the other into the sleeves until it was finally in place. Smoothing it down over Beast's body, Oliver grimaced. "I'll tell you, buddy, I never thought I would be the type of guy to put clothes on his dog."

"Well, if it's any consolation, I think he looks adorable," Eve said behind him.

Oliver turned, and when she got a look at his face, she paled.

"Oh my God, Oliver, what happened?"

Oliver had known she was going to freak when she saw the massive bruising on his cheek, but he hadn't expected her to race toward him and reach up like she was going to touch it.

He leaned back away from her hand. "Careful, it's sore."

"Of course it is, I'm sorry," she said, dropping her hand. "What did you do?"

"What makes you think I did something?" Beast had already pushed his way between them, waiting for Eve to notice him.

Eve knelt down and stroked Beast's head, studying both dog and master behind those dark-framed glasses and shaking her head. "You two are a mess."

Beast's whole body wiggled body when she spoke, and she kissed him on his nose, earning a wet, slobbery tongue lick.

"You poor baby, you look like someone sewed your head back on," she said.

"He's lucky. The vet said if he'd kept struggling much longer, he could have hit his jugular and bled out," Oliver said.

"Well, I'm glad he's okay now," she said, standing back up. "You didn't answer me. Why do you look like you joined a fight club?"

"Bumped into a guy I don't care for, and it was just the wrong place, wrong time," he said.

"Do I need to ask what the other guy looks like?" she asked.

"He looks worse, trust me." Oliver hadn't actually seen Tate, but he remembered the blood oozing from his lip, the swelling of his eye, and the red imprints of Oliver's fists across his cheeks and nose. They had dumped him in his car after Tate knocked him out, and he'd woken up sore, sweating, and pissed at himself. At least they hadn't arrested him, though.

"Well, that's good, I guess," she said.

They stood silently for a moment, until Oliver said, "On Monday I go back to being an MP."

A shadow crossed over her face, and he saw the disappointment in her eyes. "Oh."

"Yeah." He debated telling her that he'd tried to transfer, but what good would it do? Neither one of them could change the outcome. Besides, maybe it was stupidly romantic, but if she wanted him, really wanted him the way he wanted her, then it shouldn't matter.

Fuck, he was an idiot.

Eve stepped forward, moving around Beast to be closer to him, and the sweet, fruity scent of her perfume curled around him.

"Oliver, I—"

"Eve, thank God I found you!" some guy said, rushing toward them.

Eve groaned, and Oliver wanted to tell him to get lost, but she was already turning away from him, back on the job. "What's wrong?"

"There's a vendor who isn't on the list, and we're having a hell of a time getting him to calm down."

Before she could tell him she had to go, Oliver let her off the hook. "We'll see you later."

Eve caught his eye and mouthed, *I'm sorry.*

As she walked away, Oliver resumed getting Beast ready, but he couldn't help wondering what she was sorry for.

EVE TOOK THE stage of the auditorium at eleven, smiling out at the packed house despite her apprehension. She wasn't completely alone—the auctioneer stood by the podium—but still her heart wouldn't slow down. She had never been a nervous public speaker, but this was the largest crowd she'd ever addressed, so she figured it was okay that her hands were shaking a little.

Gripping the mic with one hand, she tilted it toward her mouth and spoke.

"Good morning, everyone, and thank you so much for coming out to support our local shelters and these amazing men and women. In the United States, one-point-two million animals are euthanized every year due to overcrowding in shelters and breed discrimination. The Alpha Dog Training Program wants to decrease that number by giving dogs who may have been overlooked a second chance.

"You've probably noticed the camo-wearing canines wandering about the event today with their young handlers. These dogs are future heroes, handpicked for this program, so if you get the chance, stop and hand them one of the bones from your goody bags. They have been working hard and deserve a treat. If you haven't received a goody bag, they are located at the entrances and exits of the auditorium.

"But it's not just the canines that benefit from Alpha Dog. This program gives at-risk youth a knowledge of animal health, training, and behavior in the hopes that they might turn their lives around. The program assists with job placement, and there is even a scholarship available for a student pursuing a degree in Animal Health."

Loud applause greeted her words, and she relaxed a little.

"Today, the amazing trainers from Alpha Dog have donated their time and knowledge to you and the adorable adoptable dogs we are about to present. These dogs are from local shelters and have been given a grade of 'A' by an animal behaviorist. That means they would be an excellent addition to any home.

"In this auction, you will be bidding on a picnic lunch with both the dog and trainer, as well as a half-hour obedience lesson. All proceeds will be divided between the shelters and rescues participating in today's event. That means that one hundred percent of the money we raise goes to medical treatments, food, and shelter for the animals while they wait for their forever home. Today, we encourage you to take lots of pictures and share them on social media. Use the hashtag #pawscause and tag Alpha Dog Training Program on any platform." Taking a deep breath, she concluded, "So, what do you think? Are you ready to meet them?"

Cheers erupted from the crowd, and Eve laughed. "Well, all right, then. Our first cute canine is Thor, who is accompanied by Alpha Dog's head search-and-rescue trainer, Sergeant Dean Sparks."

As Sparks jogged onto the stage with a blond, medium-sized dog, Eve could almost hear the collective sigh from the women in the audience.

She grinned. "Aren't they pretty to look at?" The crowd laughed, and Eve continued, "Thor is a five-year-old golden retriever mix whose favorite pastimes are playing fetch, swimming, and having his long, golden locks brushed. He knows basic obedience and would make an awesome jogging and camping buddy. He promises to bring unconditional love and laughter to his new home and to never leave your side. As for his picnic lunch, he's chosen to share fried chicken, coleslaw, and buttermilk biscuits with the human who wins his time. Let's start the bidding at a hundred dollars."

Several paddles rose, and the auctioneer started taking the bids. As he rambled faster and faster, Eve nodded at Dean. Before the auction, she'd told the trainers to showcase their dogs by playing on their strengths. According to the shelter, Thor was quite the ham and, along with his basic training, could do a few fun tricks, one of which was playing dead.

"Bang, bang," Dean said loudly, pointing his finger like a gun at Thor. Thor immediately fell and rolled onto his back, lying completely still but for his open mouth and lolling tongue. The audience laughed, and a collective "aw" rose up among the flurry of bids. Finally, a woman in her mid-forties won Thor and Dean for seven hundred and fifty dollars.

"Fantastic showing, guys!" Eve shifted Thor's index card to the back of the stack and announced the next dog and trainer team.

As the auction progressed, she found herself getting into a rhythm, and even the trainers were strutting their stuff, cracking the audience up. When Megan escorted her dog out onto the stage, they did a whole bit where every time she talked to the dog, a big, beautiful husky named Siber, she would vocalize back at her. The audience was in stitches, and they went for nearly six hundred.

Eve turned to the last index card and stumbled a bit on the introduction as Oliver stepped out onto the stage with a black-and-white pit bull mix named Daisy. Now, he was going to be auctioned off to the highest bidder, and there was nothing she could do about it.

It's just a picnic. No big deal. They'll eat, talk, train, and say good-bye. Besides, you were the one who couldn't open your mouth and tell him how you feel, so really, it serves you right.

Clearing her throat, she awkwardly tried to recover from her long pause. "Accompanying Sergeant Martinez is Daisy, who would love nothing better than to find a home where she can lay under your feet all day, getting belly and ear rubs until the cows come home. Daisy wants her new family to know that she loves dancing, tea parties, and especially Channing Tatum movies." More laughter. "We'll start the bidding at one hundred dollars."

Eve nearly scowled at the amount of women's hands that shot up into the air and fought the urge to say something discouraging, like Oliver had halitosis or smelled like onions. But she wasn't stupid or impulsive. She'd look crazy, and it would only embarrass Oliver, which was the last thing she wanted.

The bidding seemed to last forever, and when it was over, a small, gleeful laugh escaped her when she saw the winner was an older woman with silver hair. Eve glanced toward Oliver, who gave her a wry smile, and her face flamed. Did he know why she had laughed?

Turning away, she addressed the crowd. "Thank you so much for coming out and supporting this great cause. Winners, please come to the table at the side of the stage to make your payment, and as for everyone else, please enjoy the rest of today's entertainment."

Eve released the mic, and as she passed by Oliver, she slowed to ask, "Where's Beast?"

"He's cooling his heels with Best, who had to deal with a situation with one of the kids."

"Is everything okay?" she asked.

"Yeah, it's fine."

"Woo-hoo, Sergeant Martinez!" the older woman who had won Oliver called from the payment table, and Eve noticed a younger woman standing next to her, looking embarrassed.

"I better go greet my date," he said.

"I'll go with you." Why was she so curious, damn it? "I need to make sure there aren't any problems."

They headed over to his winner, and Eve stood back a little to listen.

"Young man, I want you meet my granddaughter, Abigail. She is having problems with her dog, and I thought maybe you could help," the older woman said.

Eve snuck a glance at Abigail, a pretty, fresh-faced blonde with a shy smile and big blue eyes, and tried not to panic.

"Oh, and she's single," the older woman said slyly.

Son of a bitch!

Chapter Eleven

AFTER THE PICNIC, Oliver walked Abigail and Daisy over to the adoption tent and shook Abigail's hand. He had enjoyed the food and she was nice, but even if a certain raven-haired woman hadn't already overhauled his heart, nothing was going to happen with her.

"Good luck with Daisy," Oliver said. During their hour, Abigail had fallen in love with the gentle pit bull and decided to adopt her.

"Thank you so much," Abigail said, patting Daisy's head. "I think it's going to be a good match. I appreciate your time. I know my grandmother can be a little nuts."

"No, she is hilarious," he said. "Reminds me of my *abuela*."

"Well, good. It was nice meeting you," she said.

"You, too."

Oliver took off toward the gym where Best had said to meet him. Oliver's duties were over for the day, and he was supposed to drive up to his parents' for the weekend. They lived up in Mendocino, and it had been a while since he'd visited, so he figured he was due.

But before he left, he needed to get Eve alone and talk to her. Things were too confusing between them, made more so by her mixed signals and her father's threats. He needed to know if what they had was worth fighting for or whether it was all in his head.

As if his mind had conjured her, Oliver saw her standing with Beast, feeding him treats and crooning to him.

"Did you steal him from Best?" Oliver asked.

"Actually, he had an errand to run and asked if I'd watch Beast," she said.

"Well, that was nice of you." Oliver knelt down, running his hand over Beast's head as the dog wiggled and tried to lick him.

"I actually wanted to talk to you about something," Eve said. She was twisting Beast's leash up in her hands and seemed nervous about something.

"What's that?" Oliver asked.

"I was wondering if I could ask you out on a proper date," she said swiftly. "Maybe tonight?"

Oliver's heart exploded, hitting his rib cage with a force that stole his breath. He had hoped and prayed but hadn't really been sure she'd felt the same way. "What happened to your policy about guys like me?"

"I thought maybe I could make an exception for someone I like-like." She offered him a small smile, but he kept his face neutral.

"I don't know if I should get involved with a woman who doesn't respect my career choice," he said.

"A valid point. I could have said and explained my views better, but I can sometimes be a clod. But I was hoping you'd overlook my stupidity this once and give me one teeny tiny date."

Suddenly, an idea struck him, and he grinned evilly. "Yeah, I'm not really a *teeny tiny* kind of guy. I like to go big in everything I do."

"Okay, so what do you suggest?"

Oliver stood up and grabbed her free hand, sliding his fingers between hers. "I was thinking you could come with me now."

"Where?" she asked.

"I'm going to visit my parents for the weekend," he said, pulling her closer. "And I want you to come with me."

It was the craziest idea he'd ever had, but if it meant an entire weekend with Eve, away from all the reasons they shouldn't be together, he was willing to go a little insane.

Eve blinked at him, shock written all over her face. "Wait, no. To your parents' place?"

"Why not? You could get someone to handle the rest of the fund-raiser, and I've got room," he said.

"But...I was thinking like dinner and a movie," she said hesitantly. "Where do your parents live, anyway?"

"Mendocino. Ever been?"

"No," she said.

"It's about four hours north and beautiful. You'll like it. There are forests and beaches and hippies."

"Four hours?"

"Hey, you never said how long the date had to be," he said. Circling his arms around her waist, he placed his mouth next to her ear and teased, "Besides, this will give us a chance to really get to know each other. Who knows, after this weekend, we might decide we actually hate each other."

Eve hesitated, and he read the doubt in her eyes, sure she was about to say no.

"Okay. But I need ten minutes to get things squared away, and then I've got to go home and pack."

Oliver hadn't known he'd been holding his breath until it whooshed out shakily.

"I'll wait as long as it takes."

It HADN'T TAKEN long for Eve to find Megan, and when Eve had made her request, she'd gotten the reaction she expected.

"I'm sorry, can you speak into my good ear?" Megan said. "Because I'm pretty sure you just said you're taking off on a spontaneous, romantic adventure and want to leave me here to handle your crap."

Eve held her binder and planner out to Megan. "Here is everything you need to run this thing. Everyone has been paid and knows to break down at four. You just have to stand around and look pretty."

"It sounds like you're dumping an assload of responsibility on me and expecting me to do that charming Vanna White thing *you* do." Megan waved her hand along the length of her body. "Do I look like Vanna?"

"No, you look like my best friend, my only hope, and basically my everything," Eve said. "Please, I promise that if you ever get the chance to run off with a guy, I will do everything in my power to help!"

"I'm holding you to that," Megan said. With a sigh, she held out her hands for Eve's stuff.

"Thank you, thank you, thank you." Eve gave her a crushing hug.

"I expect every last gory detail, and you're buying my coffee for a month," Megan yelled, but Eve was already running toward the parking lot.

"Totally worth it!" Eve shouted over her shoulder. Frustrated with her heels, she kicked them off and picked them up, running barefoot across the grass until she made it to the edge of the parking lot. There was no way she was going to risk slicing the bottom of her feet on a rock or glass, so she slipped the heels back on and maneuvered as fast as she could to her car.

The incredibly nervous, neurotic side of her was clawing up her insides, trying desperately to give her every reason why this was completely crazy, but it was futile. Every other emotion was being outweighed by the extreme, over-the-moon happiness soaking her entire being.

Oliver was serious about her, there was no doubt. He was definitely not the type of guy to bring home every girl he was interested in to meet his parents.

Did she still have her worries and reservations? Yes, but for one weekend, she was going to put them on the back burner and live. Just be.

She could do that without her planner, right?

Eve saw Oliver leaning against his car, which was parked next to hers, and a smile so wide it hurt spread across her face.

She was definitely going to give it a shot.

AN HOUR LATER, Oliver sat in the car with Beast waiting for Eve to grab some things from her apartment. But she was taking a long-ass time. Pulling the keys out of the ignition, Oliver stepped out, reaching back in for Beast's harness and leash. They walked up the steps, and he knocked on the door she'd gone into.

No answer.

Trying the knob, he found it unlocked and pushed the door open.

Considering how immaculately dressed and groomed Eve always was, he was surprised to find that her apartment looked like a tornado had blown through it and left a couple frat brothers behind to create more chaos. Clothes covered nearly every surface. An empty bottle of wine lay on top of the coffee table along with several diet-soda cans. Take-out containers were scattered across the kitchen counters, and he could have sworn he saw something growing on some of the dirty dishes popping up out of the sink.

A fluffy black-and-white cat came out from behind the couch, took one look at them, and arched its back, hissing and growling with a high-pitched whine. Beast wiggled his body in response, and Oliver heard a crash in the other room. "Everything okay?"

"Shit," Eve said. A few seconds later, she peeked her head out of what must have been her bedroom. "What the heck are you doing in here?"

"You were taking so long I wanted to tell you to shake a leg, but now that I've seen your apartment, I gotta say—"

"Nothing! You will say nothing." She ducked her head back into her bedroom and reappeared a moment later with a large suitcase, a tote, and some kind of little black bag.

"You know we're coming back Sunday, right?"

"Yes, I know that, but I couldn't make up my mind." Oliver bit back a grin noticing that she seemed a little frazzled at him being there.

"You weren't kidding about the bras and dishes," Oliver said, only teasing.

"I know, I am the worst housekeeper in the world, which is why I pay someone to stop by once a week and clean for me."

Oliver laughed. "Hey, no judgment here. Being a good housekeeper is not one of *my* 'like-like' requirements."

Oliver could tell his reassurances weren't making her feel any better, and he walked over to her. Snaking his free arm out and around her waist, he ducked his head to catch her eye. "Hey." When she finally looked up at him with those mossy green eyes, he smiled. "Honestly, I don't care."

"Come on, you care," she said. "Everyone else does."

Vulnerability. It was in the way she avoided his gaze. Seeing it on his usually self-assured Eve was unsettling.

"You hate to clean, and I like to start fights. We both got crap that would send other people screaming, but we're both still here." Kissing her hard and fast, he dropped his forehead to hers and stared through her glasses into her eyes. "So let's grab your shit and get this show on the road."

He released her to grab her suitcase and wheeled it behind him as Beast led the way out of the apartment. "Who's going to watch your cat?"

"I texted Megan to stop in and check on her, but she has an automatic waterer and feeder that usually last her a week," Eve said.

"Aren't you worried about the fund-raiser falling apart without you?" he asked when they reached the car.

"Actually, no. I planned everything down to the wire, and Megan is competent. Granted, she's probably furious with me, but I'll make it up to her," Eve said.

Oliver opened the trunk, and once everything was loaded inside, he slammed it shut with a grin. "You ready?"

"As I'll ever be."

Chapter Twelve

"So, ARE YOU going to tell me why you got into a fight?" Eve asked.

They had been on the road for several hours, and although they had talked about Beast, their childhoods, and their first kisses, Oliver didn't want to answer this particular question. Not just because he didn't want to hurt Eve's feelings, but also because he didn't want to give her any more reasons why they shouldn't be together. He was still shocked that she'd agreed to come with him in the first place and, more to the point, that he had asked. His mom was going to go nuts; he'd never brought a girl home, at least, not since high school, and his mom had hated Rochelle.

Somehow, he got the feeling his mom was going to love Eve, though.

"I bumped into Tate and that guy Andy outside your dad's office. You met Tate, he's a dick. He just started mouthing off, so I popped him. Andy got a hold of me long enough for Tate to knock me out and dump me at my car."

"Why were you at my dad's office?" she asked.

He almost told her about wanting to stay at Alpha Dog, but what good would it have done? Her dad had made up his mind, and the last thing he wanted to do was create a rift between them.

"It was how I found out I was going back into rotation on Monday," he said.

"Oh." She didn't say anything else, and he figured she probably didn't want to talk about his job.

After a moment of silence, she changed the subject. "Tell me about your parents. Are your sisters going to be there?"

"No, they're both married now. Margie lives in Texas with her husband and twin sons, and Luz is in San Diego. Her husband is a jarhead, but I don't hold that against him."

"I can't imagine living far away from my mom after I had kids," Eve said.

"My mom and Margie love each other but are so much alike that they butt heads constantly. My mom stayed with her for a few months after the twins were born, and Margie's husband said it was like a war zone every day. Luz and I are more like our dad. He calls my mom his little spitfire because she is barely five feet tall, but when she gets mad, watch out. Once, when I was a teenager and had smarted off about something, she actually took her shoe off and started chasing me around the room with it. When she couldn't catch me, she threw it at me."

"Oh my God," Eve said, laughing.

"Oh, yeah. My mom doesn't take crap, and she is crazy protective."

"She sounds amazing," Eve said.

"My dad definitely thinks so. He was raised on the East Coast, and instead of going to college like his family wanted, he joined the army and got stationed in Texas. He met my mom on a weekend pass and married her. When my dad got out, he joined the police department, and my mom stayed home with us for a few years, picking up waitressing jobs at night when my dad was home. When we were in school all day, my mom started waitressing full time, and on weekends we always did things as a family. It taught me how to be responsible and take care of myself."

Oliver stopped talking and noticed that Eve had become really quiet. Reaching across to take her hand, he squeezed it gently. "Hey, you okay?"

"Just nervous," she said.

"It's okay, *dulzura*," he said. "They're going to love you."

AS OLIVER PARKED the car in front of a large home surrounded by trees, Eve had a hard time catching her breath. She'd met a few boyfriends' parents before, but this was different. She had never experienced roiling nausea at the thought of someone's parents hating her, had never really been worried about impressing people in general, but these people had created Oliver—amazing, funny, handsome Oliver—and she wanted them to like her.

Correction: She *needed* them to like her.

"We're here," Oliver said.

Giant redwood pines surrounded the dark brown house with tan trim and the colorful flower beds drawing attention to the brick walkway. The heavy oak front door had an intricate beveled-glass window with a pine tree in the center. Beyond the house, Eve caught glimpses of blue water and couldn't wait to see the full impact of the view.

"It's beautiful," Eve breathed.

"Yeah, my mother adores it. When my grandfather died, it turned out he hadn't completely written my parents off the way they'd thought. He hadn't spoken to my father in years, so the inheritance he left them came as a surprise. My dad was always good with money, and by the time he'd retired, he'd tripled the money my grandfather had left him, so he started looking for a beautiful place with mild weather. He got this place for a relatively good price when the market crashed a few years ago." Oliver grinned at her across the top of the car. "Wait until you see the view."

Eve had barely shut her door when an older man and woman came out of the house. The woman squealed and rushed toward Oliver, hugging him fiercely before cupping his bruised face in her hands. "Ah, *mijo*, what have you done to yourself?"

"Hey, Mom, don't worry about it," Oliver said, his cheeks rosy red. Eve couldn't stop the giddy bubbling in her chest as she watched him greet his mom and then his father. She'd already known he was a good guy who loved his family, but seeing it in person was different.

"Mom, Dad, this is Evelyn Reynolds, the friend I told you was coming," Oliver said. Eve shot him a surprised glance, and he added, "I called them while I was waiting for you to pack."

She came around the front of the car to greet them, holding her hand out. "Hi, Mr. and Mrs. Martinez. It's so nice to meet you. You can call me Eve."

"Eve, it's a pleasure to have you. You may call me Edward." Oliver's dad took her hand in his and squeezed it.

"Oh, it is so nice to meet you." Oliver's mom pulled her in for a hug. "I am Maria. I had given up on my Oliver ever bringing a girl home."

"Don't listen to her," Oliver said. When Eve caught his eye, he made the crazy symbol by his head, making her giggle.

"Come in. We'll leave the men to get the bags, and I'll show you the house. Are you thirsty? I can get you something to drink."

"I am fine, thank you," Eve said. Oliver's mother laced her arm through Eve's and led her inside. The house was an open floor plan, with the kitchen and living and dining rooms flowing into one another. It was three times as big as her apartment. The beautiful wood walls of the living room were adorned with art and photographs, and a large bay window showed off a breathtaking ocean view. The dining room had a long table with eight chairs. On the wall hung an abstract painting with vibrant colors that drew out the red cushions on each chair.

And the kitchen…Well, if Eve ever learned to cook, this would be her dream kitchen, with an enormous island in the center and ample cabinet space. She could put a thousand dishes in all the cupboards and never have to do dishes again. Eve bit back a laugh at the thought, but endless dish storage aside, it was an extraordinary home.

"Oliver will have to take you down to the beach and into town while you're here. Is this your first time in Mendocino?" Maria asked.

"Yes, it is. Your home is gorgeous."

"Thank you. It's larger than our old house but is actually only two bedrooms and two bathrooms, while our first home was three bedrooms and one bathroom. We do have a cabin and a pull-out couch, though, so we can host quite a few people, which is great when our kids come to visit." Maria's smile was kind as she added, "Especially when they bring guests."

"I hope I am not imposing, it was so last minute—"

"Of course you are not an imposition. It is nice to have another woman around to talk to. Otherwise, my son and husband try to run roughshod all over me."

"Don't listen to her, Eve," Oliver said from the doorway. He had his duffle and her smaller bags. Beast sat at his side, sniffing a plant by the door.

"Oliver Manuel Martinez, if that dog pees in my house, you're going to be in trouble," Maria said.

"He's housebroken, Mom," Oliver said. "Should I put our stuff in the cabin?"

"You may put *your* things in the cabin, but I've already made up the guest room for Evelyn." Maria's chin was in the air, and Eve thought it was adorable that the woman seemed to be protecting her virtue.

"Are you serious? I am a grown-ass man—"

"And I am your mother. This is my home, and if you don't like it, you are more than welcome to find a hotel."

"I could sleep on the sofa bed," Oliver said.

"And have you try to sneak down the hall into her room when you think I'm sleeping? Don't think I don't know all your tricks, *mijo*."

"You are being ridiculous," Oliver said.

Eve bit back a laugh at their banter. Oliver's mother reminded Eve of her dad when he was laying down the law, and the best way to get on her dad's side was to agree with him.

"I'm good in the guest room," Eve said.

Maria looked at her in approval, and Oliver scowled, mouthing *traitor*.

Laughing, Eve went to collect her bags from the men and whispered in Oliver's ear, "I never go all the way on the first date, anyway."

OLIVER SAT BACK in his chair, stuffed full of his mother's enchiladas and already wanting to escape his parents with Eve. He hadn't really imagined his mother would enforce her only-married-people-share-a-room policy, but there was nothing he could do about it.

"That was so good, thank you," Eve said, groaning. "I don't know if I'm going to be able to move!"

"Really?" Oliver said. "Because I was thinking we could take a walk down to the beach and check out the moon."

"Yes, you two go and enjoy yourselves," Maria said.

Oliver stood up, ready to get out of there and be alone with Eve.

"Let us clean up dinner, Maria. You go put your feet up. Oliver can help me put things away," Eve said.

Oliver almost groaned aloud, until he saw his mother's face light up with delight and approval. "No, you are our guest—"

"I insist," Eve said.

His mother didn't put up much of a fight, though, and escaped to the living room. His dad sat down in his easy chair and flicked on the TV, clicking through the channels. Oliver smiled when he heard his mother tell him to go back to a romantic movie. And although his father sighed loudly, he did as she asked.

Oliver admired his parents and the way they compromised to make each other happy. That compromise was what he'd always been on the lookout for, for himself: a woman who kept him on his toes. Ultimately, though, he just wanted to be happy.

Hopefully he could have that with Eve, if he could just get her alone.

Eve gathered the dishes from the table and walked around the kitchen island to the sink while he followed behind with the enchiladas.

"Are you trying to avoid me?" he asked, whispering so his parents wouldn't hear.

Eve's shocked expression told him all he needed to know. "No! I'm a guest and am trying to make a good impression on your parents. Just because I'm messy in my own apartment doesn't mean I was raised by wolves."

"Actually, your dad is more like a hungry grizzly bear—"

Oliver jumped when Eve slapped him with a dish towel. "Be nice," she said.

Coming up behind her, he put both hands on the edge of the sink, boxing her in. "I'm trying to be very nice, but you aren't giving me a chance," he said against the side of her neck.

And got an elbow to his ribs for his efforts. "Behave. Your parents are right there."

Oliver glanced across the large, open room to where his parents sat, engrossed in their movie. "Exactly why I'm trying to get us out of here," he grumbled.

"Well, the faster we clean the kitchen, the sooner we can go on that romantic moonlit walk." She handed him the same towel she'd whacked him with. "I'll scrub, you dry."

"Aye-aye, captain. And by the way, I never said it was going to be romantic." He leaned his hip against the counter and teased, "You shouldn't go putting words in my mouth."

Suddenly he got a face full of water from the sink sprayer. Wiping his face off, he locked eyes with Eve, who dropped the sink sprayer back into place. Giggling and backing away toward the side of the island, she gasped, "That should teach you some respect."

Oliver's lips twitched, but his tone came out a dark, gravelly threat. "You're dead."

With lightning speed, he lunged for her, but she made it to the other side of the large, marble island. He kept coming, and she took off, squealing and circling the granite square, not slowing even when Beast bounded to his feet, barking and joining in the game.

The third time around, Oliver managed to catch her when she went for the sink's hose again and wrestled her arms to her sides. She was breathless with laughter, and he wanted to kiss her, to feel her arms wrap around him and pull him into her body.

"Children!" his dad called from the living room. "We are watching a movie. Try to keep it down."

Eve pulled out of his embrace, blushing, and Oliver cursed his dad for interrupting their moment.

Ten minutes later, the kitchen was shiny and the dishwasher loaded. Before something else came up, Oliver took her hand and tugged. "We're going for a walk. Can Beast stay with you, Mom?"

At the mention of his name, Beast looked up from his comfortable spot covering Oliver's mom's feet in front of the couch and laid his head back down again.

"Sure, he's just keeping my feet warm. Be careful and take a flashlight," his mother called.

Oliver grabbed one and had almost made it to the door when his dad said, "And you might want to wear a sweatshirt or jacket."

"I didn't bring one," Eve whispered.

"I've got an extra." Even if he'd only had the one, he would have gone without just to get out of there. As they walked the short distance to his cabin, Oliver was surprised when Eve volunteered to wait outside.

"Are you afraid my mom's going to catch you in my cabin and get mad?"

"Yep, most definitely," she said.

Oliver chuckled as he went in and grabbed the sweat-shirts. He handed her one, and once it was all zipped and in place, he held his hand out for hers.

"Come on. The trail's just this way."

Chapter Thirteen

EVE KICKED OFF her shoes the minute they hit sand, loving the feel of the cold, wet grains under her heels and between her toes. It had been a long time since she'd been to the beach, mainly because it was hard to coordinate a vacation to the coast with her friends, but this was heaven.

Made better by the man holding her hand and leading her toward the water.

"We're not going in, right?" Eve looked out over the midnight black water and could just imagine what lurked below the surface.

"Nah, too cold." Oliver sat down in the sand and pulled her down between his legs. Eve relaxed and snuggled back into him as he circled her in his arms. He didn't try for more than that, and part of her was disappointed after all the effort he'd gone through to get her alone.

"It's beautiful here," she said.

"Yeah, I love it. Maybe someday I'll retire here," Oliver said.

"Did you ask for the Sacramento post to be close to them?" she asked.

"I wanted it, but you know as well as I do that they move you where they want you, without your permission."

His comment sent cold water through her veins, reminding her that he could be ripped from her any-time.

"Where'd you go just now?" he asked.

"I was just thinking that everything I thought I wanted went out the window the minute you got into my car the day we met," she said honestly.

His lips found the side of her neck. "I, for one, am happy that you didn't kill me. Your driving is seriously terrifying, *dulzura*."

"You know, following up an insult with an endear-ment does not make it okay," she said.

"Come on, admit it." He trailed his lips softly across her neck, and tingles raced down her spine. "It's hot when I drop a little *español* on you."

"Please, like I'm one of those girls who goes weak in the knees over accents and foreign languages."

Oliver placed his mouth at the shell of her ear and spoke softly, "*Tú me vuelves loco.*"

You drive me crazy. Eve clenched her thighs together, trying to ignore the throb between them. "I feel nothing."

"*Te quiero besar.*"

I want to kiss you.

"Go ahead. Your sultry words and deep voice have no effect on me."

Oliver's hands trailed down over her stomach, stopping to rest on her thighs. His fingers drew slow, languid circles over her jeans, burning through the fabric and onto her skin. *"Quiero hacerte el amor."*

I want to make love to you.

"Oh, God." Eve turned in his arms and reached her hand behind Oliver's neck. Before he could resist, she yanked his mouth down to hers and kissed him with every pent-up, almost, could-have-been moment they'd shared but never finished.

It didn't surprise her that Oliver didn't leave her in control long but rolled with her until she was under him, his big body pressing her into the cold sand. His lips and tongue moved with hers, and she couldn't get close enough to him. Her hands snaked under the back of his shirt, and his warm skin against her palm was smooth, tight, and ripping with muscles.

Eve wasn't the most experienced woman, having only been with three men, but with Oliver she didn't feel nervous or awkward, like she had to play a part. She was hungry, raw, and craving him—every part of him.

"God, Eve, I want you so bad." His tone was rough with desire, his reaction to merely her kiss causing her passion to boil over.

"I want you, too," she said.

"Just not here," he said.

His words hit her hard, and she pulled back from his kiss. "What?"

He adjusted her glasses, which had been knocked a little sideways during their kiss, and stared down at her, hard. "Baby, I don't want our first time together to be on a cold, wet beach with sand everywhere."

"Then why did you bring me down here?" she asked.

"Well, I thought I was being romantic, showing you the sky and the ocean at night—whoa!"

Eve grabbed the front of his shirt and jerked him down until they were nose to nose. "Oliver, every single time I think this is going to happen, something comes up and we've put a pin in it. I'm not in the mood to put a pin in anything tonight."

"If I take you right now, you're going to end up itchy and pissed off at me," he said, pushing himself off her.

Eve lay there, glaring up at him. "I thought the guy was supposed to be ready anytime, anywhere." Climbing to her feet, she brushed at her clothes, brushing off the sand. "I think you wanted to get me all revved up and leave me hanging because you think I'm going to break your mom's rules and sneak out to your cabin."

"Actually, I thought we could just go back there and get cleaned up—"

"Oh, no! No, I am not rewarding you for devious behavior." Eve gathered up her shoes and started back toward the staircase, her calves screaming against the new terrain and her angry walk.

"Eve, you are being ridiculous. We are adults, for God's sake, and if I want to bring you to my parents' for the weekend, then damn it, we can share a bedroom!"

She stopped at the edge of the stairs and bent over to put on her shoes. "I'll tell you one thing, Oliver Martinez. The next time you want to seduce me in Spanish, you better be prepared to follow through."

OLIVER TOSSED AND turned in bed hours later, cursing his mother and her stupid rules. And Eve, too, for getting mad at him because he was concerned with her comfort. Here he was being a good guy, and he got punished for it. *Women.*

"This is bullshit," he growled aloud.

Climbing out of bed, he left the cabin and made his way up to the main house. He tried the knob and realized his parents had locked the door. "Shit."

He was feeling around in the dark, trying to find the spare key when suddenly the porch light flipped on and his mother opened the door. "*Mijo*, what are you doing?"

"Uh…" Damn it, how did she still manage to make him feel like a kid getting caught after curfew? "I'm hungry."

His mother didn't look like she believed him, but she waved him inside. "Come in."

Oliver followed her inside and sat at the table.

"I know you didn't come over here for a late-night snack, but I'll overlook it because I wanted to talk to you, anyway." She opened the fridge and pulled out sandwich fixings, making his sandwich while they talked.

"You know this whole separate-rooms thing is old school, right?" he said.

"I know that is your opinion. Do you think I want to listen to you have sex in my house?"

"We could have stayed in the cabin for Chr—" He stopped himself when his mother glowered at him, a sharp knife in her hand. "Goodness' sake."

"Maybe I wanted to get the measure of your young lady. By the way, I like her very much."

"Me, too."

"Which means I have to ask...Did she give you that black eye?"

"Of course not!"

"Then did you get it because of her?"

"Why would you even ask that?"

"Why don't you answer me?"

Oliver took the sandwich and bottled water she handed him and sighed. "It wasn't because of her. I'd been having a crappy day, and I bumped into a fellow MP who made some inappropriate comments about Eve and I snapped."

"What kind of things? Have I not told you that you cannot fight every battle with your fists?"

"Believe me, Mom, you would have knocked his ass out, too."

"Does Eve have a...reputation? Is that why he was talking about her?"

"No, are you kidding me?" Oliver said angrily. "He was trying to get a rise out of me, that's all."

"But why would he care?"

Leave it to his mother to keep digging at him until he revealed all. "Anyone ever tell you you're like a dog with a bone?"

"Your father," she said. "Now, tell me why he thought he could get to you through Eve?"

Oliver sighed and ran his hands over his face. It would feel good to talk to someone about how to handle the general. He had made it pretty damn clear that he didn't want Oliver anywhere near Eve, and once he found out he'd spent the weekend with her, Oliver was a dead man.

But Oliver still thought Eve was worth whatever her dad dished out.

"The base commander is Eve's father, and Tate was giving me a bad time about it, so I punched him. I was on edge because her father had stuck me in this publicity position for this new outreach program, which is where I ended up meeting Eve. In spite of her father, I wanted to be with her. But Eve doesn't date military guys, so I went to the general and asked him if I could be transferred permanently to the Alpha Dog Training Program. He told me no and that if I didn't stay away from his daughter, I'd find myself transferred to a completely different base." Oliver pushed the sandwich away and laughed bitterly. "And then we came here, and you were pretty much just one more person telling me I couldn't be with her. And it just sucks, Mom, you know?"

His mother was quiet, almost too quiet. He looked up and caught the shine of tears in her eyes. "Do you love her?"

The truth came tumbling out before he even thought about it. "Yeah, I think so. I mean, we haven't known each other that long, but it doesn't seem to matter."

"Pshaw, there is no right time for love to grow. It can be instantaneous or it can take years. I knew I loved your father after our second date; I just had to wait for him to catch up."

"I just don't know how to get her dad to trust me with her," Oliver said.

"As you've said yourself, you are both grown-ups. What her father thinks doesn't matter. It's her life."

"Thanks, Mom, for the pep talk. I kind of needed it."

"Any time, *mijo*," she said. "Now, finish your sandwich and get out of my house."

EVE CLOSED HER door and leaned her head back against the solid wood. She'd heard Oliver's voice in the house and almost run out to greet him, until she'd heard his mom. She had just been about to go back to bed, but then he'd said her name; unable to resist, she'd cracked the door enough to listen.

God, her dad had gone too far. Oliver had been willing to give up being an MP for her and never said a word? Come Monday, she was going to have a long talk with her dad about making her decisions for her. It might have been done to protect her, but she'd almost missed out on being with Oliver.

And that dick Tate? Man, was she glad Oliver had broken his face.

Then Oliver had admitted that he thought he loved her, and the knots in her stomach had loosened. She'd been struggling with the *L* word herself, knowing logically that it was too soon, but emotionally it was there, at the tip of her tongue every time she was with him.

She had fallen in love with a military man. A man like her father: honorable, kind, a little bit stubborn, and with some jackass tendencies, but still completely wonderful. Oliver and his mother were still talking when Eve got an idea.

An exciting, wonderful, awful idea.

Climbing onto the bed, she unlocked and opened the window over it. The drop was only about three feet, easy peasy. Quietly, she pushed out the screen, being sure not to damage it, and slowly swung out of the window before dropping to the ground. Once the screen was replaced, she walked to Oliver's cabin and hurried inside.

And waited. Waited. And waited some more.

And then she heard the thud of the front door as he left the main house and the crunch of gravel under his feet. Sitting on the edge of the bed, she held her breath until the door opened.

When Oliver saw her, he stalled for a second, just staring at her.

"Get in here," she whispered.

Oliver stepped into the cabin and shut the door behind him. "What are you doing? What happened to respecting my mother's rules?"

Without a word, she took off her glasses and laid them on the nightstand, blinking as her vision blurred. Closing her eyes, she then slowly reached down and gathered the edge of her T-shirt. Before she lost her nerve, she pulled the shirt over her head and tossed it to the floor.

Opening her eyes again, she stood. "I heard you talking to your mom...about Tate and my dad." Eve took several steps across the room and brought Oliver's hands to her lips. "And I needed to see you."

Oliver didn't move for several moments, then suddenly, she was being lifted against him. "Sorry, I didn't hear anything after your shirt came off."

Eve laughed, wrapping her arms around his shoulders as he tumbled her back on the bed. Hovering over her, Oliver trailed his fingers along her cheek and chin. "So, did you also hear me tell my mom how I feel about you?"

"Yes," she said.

"I meant every word."

"I wouldn't be here if I thought you didn't," she said.

This time, when Oliver kissed her, pressing her down into the mattress, Eve wasn't letting anything come between them, not even their clothes. As she helped Oliver discard his shirt, her gaze devoured the muscles she uncovered but had never seen. He stood up off the bed and was reaching for the waistband of his sweats when she saw the bruising on his ribs and frowned.

"Where did you get those bruises?"

"Tate. He likes to kick a guy while he's down."

Eve wanted to clobber Tate and vowed to make him pay for hurting her man. "Are you too sore?"

"Hell, no," he said. As he removed the rest of his clothes, she drank in his hard body and stiff cock jutting upward.

Sliding to the edge of the bed, she reached out and ran her fingertips gently over his ribs and abdomen, before her lips followed along. Finally taking his hips in her hands, she leaned over, pressing a sweet kiss to the end his cock. The sound of his groan was like music, and opening her mouth, she took him deeper, reveling in the salty taste of his skin.

Before she could protest, Oliver put his hands around her arms and lifted her off of him. "I want to kiss you," he said.

And then his mouth covered hers and she felt his fingers deftly untying the drawstring of her pajama pants. Lightning sparked across her hips and thighs as he pushed them down, his fingers and palms running over her body until she was left in her panties and her pajamas were locked around her knees.

Oliver gently pushed her back on the bed and pulled her pants the rest of the way off before settling between her thighs, dropping a soft, gentle kiss above her panty line.

"*Hazme el amor,*" Eve said.

Oliver looked down at her, his eyes shining in the cabin light, and she trailed her hand over the side of his face, repeating herself again, only this time, in English.

"Make love to me."

Chapter Fourteen

ONCE HE PULLED off Eve's panties, Oliver stared down at her, wanting to touch her everywhere at once.

"You're so beautiful," he said.

"I bet you say that to all the girls," she teased.

Oliver reached out and squeezed her side, delighted when she laughed and squirmed away from his hand. "Must you cheapen the moment?"

"I'm sorry, please!"

"At least I know from now on how to best you." He wiggled his fingers for emphasis, but instead of tickling her again, he flattened his palms against her stomach. He slid them up until they rested beneath her breasts, cupping them tenderly.

"I feel a little like you're studying me," she said.

Oliver shook his head and lowered his mouth to the tip of her breast. "I'm worshiping you. There's a difference."

His closed his lips over her hardened nipple, sucking and running his tongue over it until she was arching against him, holding the back of his head in her hands.

Oliver continued to caress, stroke, and kiss her everywhere he could reach, the soft moans and cries making it hard not to rush, to bury himself inside her and seek satisfaction.

But he wanted more for this, for them.

Because he'd never been in love before, and the woman he loved deserved more.

"Oliver…"

She whispered his name as his mouth found the skin of her inner thigh and he kissed his way up to the center of her. "Yes?"

"You're making me crazy."

"That's the point, *dulzura*."

He didn't give her a chance to answer; instead, he put his mouth on her and thrust his tongue forward, seeking the tiny nub of her clit. Using his hands, he worked her over thoroughly, pushing and pulling, licking and nibbling until he felt her begin to tremble under his mouth. When her sweet cry of release broke over him, he kissed his way up her torso, grinning when he reached her rapidly rising and falling chest.

"Oh…my…God."

"Now, now, no need to flatter me."

Breathless laughter escaped her. "You are so cocky."

"Speaking of that, I'll be right back."

EVE HAD NEVER had fun during sex. She'd never teased, joked, or flirted. Sex was…awkward unless you really knew the person. She tended to clear her mind, close her eyes, and never speak.

But with Oliver, it was fun on top of amazing. Even now, she had the urge to giggle as she squinted as she watched him search through his duffle for a condom, her eyes glued to his ass.

His perfect, round behind.

"Damn it!"

"No luck?" Disappointment crashed through her. She wasn't on the pill or she'd say go for it. She trusted Oliver.

More than that, she loved him.

Rolling over, she checked the drawer of the nightstand and riffled through the contents.

Nothing.

"Bathroom?" she suggested.

Oliver took off for it, and this time, Eve did start laughing.

"You know, no man likes having his dick laughed at."

Eve scooted to check the other nightstand and called, "I wasn't laughing at your dick, I was laughing at the way it—"

"Ah-ha!" Oliver slid back into the room with a foil package in his hand and wiggled his eyebrows. "Come to papi!"

"I'm not calling you"—Eve squealed as Oliver flipped off the light and, seconds later, pounced on her—"papi."

"So, we should stick with 'God,' then?" he teased. She heard the sound of the foil package opening and reached out blindly, her hand finding the muscles of his shoulder.

"Anyone ever told you that you talk too much?" she asked.

Oliver's big body shifted until he was lying on top of her, his muscular frame pressing her back. Before she had a chance to adjust, he kissed her so hard and deep that lights exploded behind her eyelids.

He broke the kiss and shifted, pressing the head of his cock against her entrance. With one more light brush of his lips across hers, he whispered, "Never."

Eve couldn't laugh, not when she could feel him push forward. She lifted her hips, moaning as he sank into her. Her eyes closed involuntarily, but instead of the nothing she usually saw during sex, her mind was filled with Oliver. Oliver's smile. His eyes. The first time he'd kissed her. Every little moment, every phone conversation, and every glance raced through her mind as he slid in and out of her in a perfect dance that cause a heavy ache inside.

And then she broke, her hips meeting his until she was light-headed and soaring. The high-pitched cries escaping her were smothered by his kiss, his tongue. She didn't want him to stop, so she slid her hands down to his ass, his perfect quarter-bouncing ass, and squeezed, pressing him into her.

Oliver took the hint and pulled back up, thrusting into her at a heightened speed, pumping her sensitive flesh until he stiffened above her, yelling his release. Still she held on until he collapsed on top of her, his chest pressing into her breasts hard as he tried to catch his breath.

Wrapping her arms around his shoulders, she caressed his skin, the wet sheen against her fingertips a turn-on. And all she could think was that this moment, right here, was worth anything that came in the future.

Because she loved Oliver Martinez.

Oliver rolled off her and kissed the side of her neck. "I'll be right back."

Eve lay there in the dark while he went to the bathroom and searched blindly for the quilt on the bed to cover herself. Without Oliver's warmth, the cabin was chilly.

Oliver came out of the bathroom and fumbled into bed with her.

"Come here, I'm cold," he said.

Smiling, she cuddled into his body, her legs entwining with his, and kissed his chest, drawing little finger hearts on the wall of muscle.

"Eve…about your dad—"

"We don't have to talk about it now. It will be okay," she said.

"Listen to me, okay?" he said. "If he does manage to get me reassigned, I want you to come with me."

"What?" she said.

"If he gets me moved to another base, I don't want to go without you."

Eve's heart thundered in her chest, happiness and uncertainty colliding. She was sure of Oliver and how she felt about him, but moving from her family, possibly thousands of miles away?

Her hand found his cheek in the darkness, and she pressed a kiss to his lips. "It would make for one hell of a second date."

OLIVER WOKE UP on his back with Eve sprawled out over him, and although the cabin was still relatively dark, sunlight was creeping through the curtains.

Kissing the top of her head, he eased out of bed to use the bathroom. After he'd asked her to follow him if he wound up being transferred, they'd lain together quietly until Oliver had heard the steady sound of her breathing. He'd had trouble falling asleep, though, wondering if she really meant what she'd said. Would she go with him? Despite how he felt about her, they hadn't been together long, and it was a lot to ask.

He went back to bed and crawled in with her, bringing her against his chilled body.

"Why are you cold?" she asked sleepily.

"Had to go to the bathroom."

"Mmm…me, too, but it's warm in here."

Oliver chuckled. "Just don't have an accident."

"Shut up," she said, slapping his chest and squinting at him. "What time is it?"

"No idea."

Suddenly she bolted upright. "Oh my God. Your mother."

"What?"

"I snuck out of her guest bedroom window like a horny teenager, and I don't think I can sneak back in."

"So, don't. In a little while, we'll head in together. She won't say a word about it. I promise."

"Maybe not to you," Eve said.

She grabbed her glasses off the nightstand and scrambled out of bed, looking around the room, and Oliver shook his head as she started gathering her clothes. "But she'll probably say something to your dad and her friends, and she'll definitely hate my guts. You have to help me sneak back in."

"What? Stop it and come here," he said. She had her underwear in place and her shirt in her hand, but he got up and grabbed her, pulling her back into his arms. "You want me to help you climb back into the guest-room window so that my mother doesn't know you snuck out here to have your way with me? All because you're afraid if she found out you find me irresistible, she might not like you? That's sweet, but certifiable."

"Please, I'll do anything you want!"

"Anything, huh?" He squeezed her against him and wiggled his eyebrows.

"Yes, pervert, anything."

"Deal," he said, lifting his hand for her to take. When she shook it, he added, "But I'm collecting now."

EVE FELL THROUGH the window onto the bed, laughing.

"Are you okay?" Oliver asked from outside.

Eve stuck her head out and nodded. "I'm good."

"This is stupid, you know that, right?"

"Come on, this is kind of romantic," she said.

Oliver replaced the screen and shook his head. "I'll see you inside."

Eve shut the window and changed her clothes. She'd showered at the cabin and now tried to towel-dry her hair so no one would notice it was wet.

Stepping out into the hallway, she bumped into Oliver's mom and Beast, who was dogging her heels.

"Good morning, Maria."

"Good morning, Eve. I trust you slept well?"

There was a sparkle in the short woman's dark eyes that made Eve swallow hard. "Yes, very well, thank you."

"I'm glad to hear it."

Eve followed her into the kitchen, where Oliver was sitting at the table with his dad, reading the paper.

"Good morning, Oliver. And how did you sleep?"

"Oh, I slept excellently, Mom." Oliver's grin was teasing, and Eve almost groaned aloud.

"Eve didn't disturb you?" Maria asked, smirking.

This time, Eve did groan and laid her head on the counter.

"Not in the least, Mom."

Kill me now.

Chapter Fifteen

OLIVER'S PHONE ALARM went off Tuesday morning at five, and as he opened his eyes, it took him a moment to remember where he was. He sat up and glanced around the room. The hall light shining through the open door revealed a floral comforter across his lap and Matilda sleeping by his feet.

Last night, after they'd arrived back at Eve's and she'd invited him up, he'd tried shutting the light off when they went to bed, but Eve had insisted it stay on. Finally, she'd admitted she was still scared of the dark, and when he'd teased her about it, he'd gotten a pillow to the face. That had led to wrestling around on her bed and dissolved into white-hot passion. At one point he'd thought they might break the bed it was squeaking so loud. When it was over, she had snuggled up against his side and whispered the sweetest words he'd ever heard.

"I love you, Oliver."

Oliver reached for his phone on the nightstand and turned off the alarm. He was tempted to skip his workout this morning, just roll back over and kiss Eve awake, but when he glanced over at her, she looked exhausted. It was no surprise with how busy their weekend had been. He still couldn't believe how fast the time had flown by.

Eve had eventually forgiven his parents for teasing her about sneaking out to see him and had even started to razz them back. His mom finally relented on letting Eve sleep in the cabin, if only to save her flower beds from being trampled. And even as Eve had blushed, Oliver grinned. He wasn't going to object.

Not when it meant he got to hold Eve all night.

When they'd said good-bye to his parents yesterday afternoon, his mother had insisted that he be good to Eve and never let her go. He'd promised he was going to do his best to keep her happy.

"Good. Because I want grandchildren before I'm too old to pick them up."

Oliver shook his head remembering, but it was funny; the thought of a future with Eve, a future that included a couple kids, didn't sound too bad.

"What the hell was that god-awful noise?" Eve grumbled next to him.

Oliver chuckled at her grouchiness. "Just my alarm. Go back to sleep."

She cracked one eye open. "What time is it?"

"Five," he said.

"Why? I thought your shift didn't start until later."

"I usually go to the gym now," he said.

"Ugh, you are disgusting. Come back to bed. Your perfect abs will hold for a few more hours," she said, reaching out to him.

Screw it. Lying back down, he pulled her against him and closed his eyes.

However, the sensation of dancing fingers working their way down his stomach dissuaded any thoughts of going back to sleep.

"I thought you were tired?"

"Not so much anymore," she said. "Besides, I thought maybe we could work out together."

As her hand wrapped around the base of his cock and squeezed, he arched up into her touch with a hoarse laugh. "I'm down with that."

It was almost noon when Eve walked into her father's office on base later that day, determined to make him see reason. She was an adult, and no matter what her father thought, she was the only one who knew what was best for her. She'd already called her mom and explained what her dad had done, denying Oliver the transfer, and her mom was on her side.

Besides, above all, her dad wanted her happy. He'd get over any misgivings he had and accept Oliver.

At least, she hoped so.

Knocking softly on his office door, Eve waited for him to say, "Come in," before she opened it. Inside, her dad was behind his desk, riffling through some papers while her mom sat in front of him, giving Eve a conspirator's grin.

Her dad's eyes widened when he glanced up and saw her. "Evie, what a nice surprise. First your mom, then you. Do you want to join us for lunch?"

"Sure, Dad," she said, "but I need to talk to you first."

Closing the door behind her, she took a breath to start, but he waved her off. "If this is about you having to leave the fund-raiser early, it's fine. The whole event was a complete success." He stood up and came around the desk to hug her. "You did good, kiddo."

"Thanks, but that's part of what I need to talk to you about." Her dad stepped back, and she took a deep breath, steeling her spine as she prepared for battle. "I want you to approve Oliver Martinez's transfer to Alpha Dog."

"Evie—"

"Please, let me explain," she said. "I am not a kid anymore, Dad. You taught me to use my head and think things through, and I do every day, but Mom…Mom taught me to go after what I want. And I want Oliver."

"He started a fight with your brother—"

"Dad, come on, you know Hank threw the first punch," she said. "Oliver was trying to help. That's the kind of guy he is. He will protect and defend others. I think part of the reason why you are so hard on him is because he's like you in so many ways. You both step up to defend people, even strangers, no matter the danger or the sacrifice. And I love that about you. It's that same quality that I love about him.

"I love him, Dad. I know it feels fast to you, but to me, it was like I just knew he was mine. That he was supposed to be with me, even though I fought it at first. He makes me laugh and accepts who I am—the honest hot mess that I am. I get that he might seem cocky sometimes, but it's okay with me." Reaching out to pat her dad's cheek, she added, "And I need you to be okay with him, too."

Her dad cleared his throat. "Eve, you can't possibly love him. It's been less than a month."

"That's the thing about being an adult, Dad. You don't get to tell me how I feel or who I should be with. I want you to give him a chance and get to know him. Maybe we could come by for Sunday dinner next weekend? You can torture him as much as you want then, and he can't escape."

Despite his scowl, Eve could tell he was relenting when he asked her mom, "Did you know about this?"

"She called me a few hours ago to tell me about her weekend. Apparently, Oliver took her to meet his parents," she said.

"His dad was army, too," Eve offered. "He was honorably discharged and has been a cop for twenty-five years. You would like him."

"Harrumph," her dad said. "I'd like to have a little talk with Sergeant Martinez. Alone."

Eve swallowed. "Why? What are you going to say to him?"

"That's between me and him," her dad said. "Now, who's hungry?"

THAT AFTERNOON, OLIVER was getting ready for work when someone knocked on his front door. Figuring it was Eve to pick up Beast, he called, "Come in."

Oliver came down the hallway, ready to give her a hello kiss, and stopped in his tracks when he found the general standing in his living room. He was stroking Beast's head slowly, but his steely gaze was locked on Oliver.

"Sir, I wasn't expecting you. How did you know where I lived?"

"I looked in your file," the general said. "I imagine you were expecting my daughter, though, am I right?"

Oliver was surprised Eve had told her dad about them without giving him a heads-up. "Actually, yes. She's going to watch Beast for me while I'm on shift."

"There's no need for that. I've already contacted Sergeant Tate and informed him you wouldn't be back," the general said.

Oliver's heart squeezed as he waited for the blow the general was about to deliver. Where would he be transferred to?

"I've reconsidered your request and decided to approve your transfer to Alpha Dog Training Program," the general said.

"You have?" Oliver felt like an idiot even saying it, but he was dumfounded. "But I thought you didn't want me anywhere near Eve."

"As it turns out, I might have been wrong about my daughter's feelings." General Reynolds didn't sound too happy about it, either. "I do want you to understand that although I am doing this for her, I don't appreciate you using her to get your way."

Before he could keep his temper in check, he exploded. "I didn't tell her about our conversation. She overheard me talking about it with someone else. You don't know me, so I can excuse your assumption, but I don't need your daughter to fight my battles for me. Sir."

The general stroked a hand over his chin and seemed to be considering him.

"Do you like to fish?" General Reynolds asked.

The question threw Oliver off, it was so out of the blue. "Yes, sir."

"Next Saturday I'd like for us to take a road trip up to Loon Lake. Just the two of us," General Reynolds said. "I never trust a man who doesn't fish."

"I'll be ready, sir." It wasn't a gold stamp of approval, but it would please Eve.

"I have one more question for you. It's about Eve," the general said.

"Okay…"

"You've seen her apartment?" General Reynolds asked.

Oliver laughed. "Yes, sir."

"Huh. I guess I was wrong," the general said.

Before he could ask the general what he was wrong about, his front door opened without even a knock and Eve stepped inside. Beast bounded over to greet her, nuzzling her hands and stomach. When she caught sight of her dad, she froze mid-pet, her expression darkening.

"Dad, what are you doing here?"

"Didn't you say I should get to know Sergeant Martinez?" the general said.

"Yes, but I thought we were doing that on Sunday," she said.

"Wait, Sunday?" Oliver asked.

Eve's cheeks turned bright red, and the general answered his question. "Oh, yes, Evie volunteered you for dinner Sunday night at our home in Carmichael. I hope that works out for you? We eat at six thirty."

"I was coming over to talk to him about it," Eve said testily.

"Sunday works for me, sir," Oliver said, shooting Eve a wink.

"Well, fine. I guess I should be going and give you two a chance to talk about all the new developments." Holding out his hand to Oliver, General Reynolds said, "I'll swing by here at five thirty on Saturday morning. Does that work for you?"

"I'll be ready," Oliver said.

"And be at the training program at oh seven hundred tomorrow."

"Yes, sir," Oliver said.

General Reynolds put a hand on Eve's shoulder as he passed and leaned over to say something in her ear, too quiet for Oliver to hear. When Eve laughed, Oliver was dying to know what was so funny.

The general gave one last wave and closed the door behind him.

"What's happening at five thirty on Saturday?" she asked.

"He's taking me fishing. I'm pretty sure fishing is code for 'killing me and dumping my body in the lake,' but I'm trying to be open to alternative theories," he said.

"Wow, he asked you to go fishing?" She sounded impressed. "I think it's safe to say that went well."

"I'm glad you thought so, because my balls were in my throat the whole time," he said.

"Believe me, my dad doesn't invite anyone to go fishing with him unless he likes them. Fishing is his sanctuary." Slowly, she closed the distance between them and wrapped her arms around his waist. "I am sorry my dad ambushed you."

"Yeah, about that. How come you couldn't give me a heads-up you were going to talk to your dad about us today?" he asked. He wasn't really mad, but he wasn't a fan of surprises either.

"Because I wanted to make sure I could bring him around to my way of thinking before I involved you."

"It seems like you handled it just fine. He approved my transfer to Alpha Dog."

Eve squealed and grabbed the back of his head, pulling his laughing mouth down to hers. The celebratory kiss soon turned hotter, and Oliver pulled back reluctantly, his cock painfully hard between them.

"As happy as I am about the transfer, you don't need to protect me, all right? I am a big boy, and if I want something bad enough, I'll make it happen."

"You could just say thank you," she teased.

"I mean it, Eve. If I'm going to earn your father's respect, you don't need to defend me or talk me up. The general and I will work our shit out without you getting involved."

"Has anyone ever told you you're bossy?" she asked.

"It's part of my charm," he said. "Do I have your word? No more fighting my battles for me?"

"Fine." Still hugging him, she looked up with a saucy sparkle in her green eyes. "I'm too happy to argue, anyway."

"Me, too." Oliver wrapped his arms around her back, nuzzling the side of her neck and inhaling. It was true; he didn't think he could be happier than he was in just this moment. His life was almost perfect, and it had all started the minute he met this amazing woman.

"I love you," she whispered.

Oliver squeezed her tighter before pulling away to gaze down at her. "I love you, too."

Her breath whooshed out like she was holding it.

"Were you afraid I wasn't going to say it back?" he asked.

"I just never imagined you saying it, so every time you do, it takes my breath away."

He cupped the side of her face, shaking his head. "*Te amo, dulzura.*"

I love you, honey.

Oliver kissed her again slowly before leaning back with a smirk. "Now that we've conquered all of our obstacles and slayed the dragon, what do you say we go back to my bedroom so I can have my way with you?"

"Megan and Allison are waiting at my place," she said apologetically.

"Will they be able to find their way out of it?" he teased.

She slapped his shoulder. "It was cleaned today, thank you very much. And besides, I thought you had to work tonight."

"Your dad took me off rotation, so I'm free."

"I'm not, so you're just going to have to wait," she said.

Oliver grabbed her when she tried to get away and without further ado, swung her up into his arms. "Text them and let them know you're going to be a few hours late."

"A few hours! No, Oliver, put me down. I have to go," she said.

He ignored her and Beast's raucous barking as he strode back toward the bedroom.

"Fine, one hour."

"No, no hour," she giggled.

"Forty-five minutes?" He stopped at the edge of his bed with his eyebrow raised as he waited for her counter.

Eve pursed her lips at him and finally said, "A half an hour and not a moment longer."

Tossing her on the bed before she changed her mind, he sighed dramatically. "I suppose it will have to do."

Eve's laughter was infectious as she pulled out her phone. While her fingers flew over the screen, he pulled off his shirt and tossed it across the room, never taking his eyes off her. His boots, socks, belt, and pants came off one at a time until he stood before her in his boxer briefs.

She set her phone on the nightstand and leaned back on her elbows. "I was so wrong about you before, Oliver Martinez."

Shucking his underwear, he put a knee on the bed, crawling up her body until he hovered over her, his lips inches from hers. "How is that, *dulzura*?"

Eve lay all the way back on the bed, and he followed her, using his arms to keep his weight off her. She reached up to caress the back of his neck, and the sensation was simply arousing.

And with the sweetest smile he'd ever seen, she stole his heart all over again.

"There is nothing I don't like-like about you."

THE CASTAWAY

Epilogue

One Year Later

OLIVER LED EVE down the beach to a rocky area he'd found a few weeks ago, holding tight to her hand as they climbed over a large boulder to a sandy alcove beyond. It was private, beautiful, and perfect for what he had planned.

"All right, you sit over here." Pushing her gently onto a smaller rock that was just the right height, he went about setting up the video camera. He'd told her they were going to make a care package for her brother, Hank, who Oliver had actually come to like over the last year. Hank had just been a little lost and lashing out, but six months ago, he'd blown his whole family away by enlisting without his dad's permission. It had been a point of contention between Hank and General Reynolds for months, but now that he was stationed overseas, the general had finally started to soften.

Oliver liked to think he'd had a hand in helping the general come around, but that might have been giving himself too much credit. Oliver had defended Hank, telling the general that he should be proud his son wanted to follow in his footsteps, and had gotten told to mind his own business. But if Oliver had learned one thing about the Reynolds clan, it was that they were stubborn but they weren't stupid.

"I think you're lying," Eve said teasingly, bringing him back to the present. "I don't think this is a video message for my brother at all. You've brought me to this secluded part of the beach to make a sex tape, haven't you?"

Oliver shook his head at her as he adjusted the video camera. "You are such a dirty girl. My mother is convinced I'm the devil in this relationship, but you are the bad influence on my innocent, fragile morals."

Eve picked up a handful of sand and pretended to throw it at him, but he knew she wouldn't. He'd been planning this moment for weeks, hoping to capture it so they could watch it again and share it with family and friends.

Just not the sex tape talk—he'd edit that out.

But the next part was definitely going to be something to see.

His grandmother's ring was burning a hole in his pocket. When he'd called his mom a few weeks ago to ask if they could use the cabin on their property, she'd asked him if he needed her mother's ring. At first, he'd been surprised she'd guessed what he was about, but then again, his mother knew him better than almost anyone.

As for the ring, he'd completely forgotten it and had been planning to just go pick one out at the mall, but this was better. Romantic, classic, and Eve was going to love it.

The last year had been eventful. Alpha Dog had become his passion, second only to Eve, who had moved in with him when her lease was up four months ago. Although Matilda had taken some getting used to and the strained relationship between she and Beast sometimes woke them up at night, their home had become a place of chaos and laughter. Eve had actually given up her housekeeper and put a chore chart in the kitchen. She'd done it as a joke, making fun of herself, but then it had turned into a competition between them. Whoever did the most chores won something from the loser, usually a back rub, but sometimes they'd get creative. The last time he'd lost, she'd made him do a striptease to a Katy Perry song, and although he had protested, the happy ending had been well worth it.

Not that she didn't drive him crazy, too, but fighting was a normal part of any relationship, and Eve, like his mother, had a stubborn, fiery side. His dad had been happy for thirty years, and Oliver knew that despite their ups and downs, Eve was the one.

And he had no intention of ever letting her get away.

"Okay, I think it's set," he said. "Do you think you could be quiet for a few moments and let me talk first?"

"He's my brother. Why do you get to go first?" she asked.

"Because if you let me go first, I'll do that thing you like when we get back to the cabin."

Her eyes lit up, and she waved her hand like a queen. "You may proceed."

Taking a deep breath, Oliver walked over to where Eve was sitting and knelt in front of her, making sure his profile was to the camera. "Evelyn Ann Reynolds…"

"Oh my *God*!" she whispered.

"I never thought I would meet my perfect match, my soul mate. You took me completely by surprise, and it doesn't matter if I have eight years left on this earth or eighty. I want to spend every single one of them with you. *Mi amor. Mi vida. Mi dulzura. Quieres casarte conmigo?*"

My love. My life. My honey. Will you marry me?

Eve couldn't speak, she was so overcome with tears. A huge lump was stuck in her throat even as she nodded, reaching out for him. She didn't stop nodding until his arms were around her and he was kissing her cheeks, her eyes, and her lips, holding her face between his hands as he devoured her.

And suddenly, she was laughing while she was kissing him.

Oliver broke the kiss and pulled a classic-set diamond ring from his pocket. Intricate engravings covered the gold band, and she held out her shaking hand for him to slide it on.

"I had no idea," she said.

"Good, because that's the way I planned it."

Eve stared down at the ring on her hand before launching herself at Oliver, knocking him back into the sand. He chuckled as she kissed him everywhere she could reach—until she lifted his shirt and kissed his rock hard abs, just above his belt buckle.

His laughter completely died as she unbuckled his belt and gave him her best sultry look. "What are you doing?"

"I'm having my way with you," she said.

"What about the sand?" he asked.

She pulled down the zipper of his pants and slipped her hand inside. "I don't care."

He groaned. "Someone could walk by."

"Not here." She pushed his pants down past his hips.

"The camera…"

Her shirt came off, and Oliver forgot what he was going to say.

Acknowledgments

SO MANY PEOPLE had a hand in writing this book, but first and foremost, I would like to thank my awesome editor, Chelsey, for all she does. My agent, Sarah, for all the behind-the-scenes work. To the cover art team at Avon, for making my beautiful, sigh-worthy cover. My husband and kids for being so supportive in this journey. To my friends, T.J. Kline and Ellie Macdonald, for talking me through the trouble spots, doubts, and insecurities. To my entire family, for reading my stuff. Cynthia Sax, Monica Murphy, and Candis Terry, thank you for allowing me to bombard you with questions and giving me your time. And a HUGE thanks goes out to my Rockers, especially their leader, Catherine Crook. You ladies make me laugh and squeal, and sometimes, when I just need to smile, I go to our group page and have a "man candy moment." Thank you for being amazing friends and readers. I love your guts.

Keep reading for a sneak peek from the next book
in Codi Gary's Men in Uniform series,

ONE LUCKY HERO

Coming April 2016 from Avon Impulse.

An Excerpt from

ONE LUCKY HERO

VIOLET DOUGLAS HAD never thought of herself as brave when it came to men, but after several drinks, she couldn't stop staring at the tall, hard-looking man across the bar.

And now she was stroking his chest like he was a big, cuddly kitten, and her fuzzy brain wanted to slide her palm lower. To find out what other muscles he was hiding under his T-shirt.

Her question seemed to surprise him for half a second, and then the corner of his mouth kicked up into a sexy half smile that tied her insides up in the best way possible.

"I didn't know you were waiting long." His voice was a deep, rumbling timbre that reminded her of Sean Connery without the Scottish accent.

"I've been watching you since you walked in," she said breathlessly. Realizing that could be construed as slightly stalkerish, she added, "I just mean that you're hard to miss."

"So are you."

Violet's cheeks warmed under his heated gaze. It was the first time she'd ever considered picking a man up in a bar, but after months of work and family drama, he looked like a desert oasis after a long dry spell.

Suddenly, a hand shot between them, and her friend Tracy Macdonald said impatiently, "Hey, I'm Tracy."

Violet sighed loudly. Tracy had been her best friend since they were in preschool, drawn together by their deep love of Play-Doh and music. Now, at twenty-four, their similarities and common interests were more complex and heartbreaking, but without her, Violet wasn't sure she'd have survived her childhood. Tracy was her rock, her lighthouse in a storm…She adored Tracy.

But as his attention turned toward Tracy and he took her petite hand in his, Violet's heart squeezed. While she was tall and gangly, Tracy was a little curve factory with gigantic blue eyes and raven's-wing black hair. Men had always been instantly drawn to Tracy, and it had never bothered Violet before.

"Dean," he said, releasing Tracy's hand swiftly. A relieved breath whooshed out when his gaze flicked away from Tracy and back to Violet's. "And you are?"

Violet slipped her hand into Dean's large, rough one and squeezed. "I'm Violet."

She couldn't tear her eyes or her hand away from him, swaying toward those hypnotic onyx eyes.

"Okay, well, nice to meet you, but I see...something, so I'm going to take off." Tracy's voice broke through their spell, and Violet released Dean's hand.

"Trace—"

"You just text me when you're ready to leave," Tracy said.

Violet knew Tracy was just giving her space, knowing full well that Violet was too responsible to go home with a stranger, but ditching her friend seemed like a dick move.

But when Violet opened her mouth to protest, Tracy opened her eyes wide, nodded her head toward Dean...

And started making kissy faced at her from behind Dean's back.

Violet laughed, and when Dean turned around, Tracy's expression was pure innocence before she turned and headed into the crowd.

"I didn't mean to run her off," Dean said.

The fact that he seemed worried about hurting Tracy's feelings made him even hotter in Violet's eyes. "That's sweet, but she's on the prowl. Most of the time, I'm the one who ends up taking off to sit in a corner."

"But not tonight," he said.

Locking her gaze with his, she shook her head. "No, not tonight."

Over the deafening hum of the bar, Dean asked, "Can I buy you another drink?"

No, you've had enough for a while.

"Yes, you can."

About the Author

An obsessive bookworm, **CODI GARY** likes to write sexy contemporary romances with humor, grand gestures, and blush-worthy moments. When she's not writing, she can be found reading her favorite authors, squealing over her must-watch shows, and playing with her children. She lives in Idaho with her family.

Discover great authors, exclusive offers, and more at hc.com.

Give in to your Impulses . . .
Continue reading for excerpts from
our newest Avon Impulse books.
Available now wherever e-books are sold.

THE BRIDE WORE RED BOOTS
A SEVEN BRIDES FOR SEVEN COWBOYS NOVEL
By Lizbeth Selvig

RESCUED BY THE RANGER
By Dixie Lee Brown

ONE SCANDALOUS KISS
AN ACCIDENTAL HEIRS NOVEL
By Christy Carlyle

DIRTY TALK
A MECHANICS OF LOVE NOVEL
By Megan Erickson

An Excerpt from

THE BRIDE WORE RED BOOTS
A Seven Brides for Seven Cowboys Novel
by Lizbeth Selvig

Amelia Crockett's life was going exactly the way
she had always planned—until one day, it wasn't.

When Mia's career plans are shattered, the always-
in-control surgeon has no choice but to head home
to Paradise Ranch and her five younger sisters,
cowboy boots in tow, to figure out how to get her
life back on track. The appearance of a frustrating,
but oh-so-sexy, former soldier, however, turns into
exactly the kind of distraction she can't afford.

He studied her as if assessing how blunt he could be. With a wry little lift of his lip, he closed his eyes and lay all the way back onto the blanket, hands behind his head. "Honestly? You were just so much fun to get a rise out of. You'd turn all hot under the collar, like you couldn't figure out how anyone could dare counter you—the big-city doc coming to Hicksville with the answers."

The teasing tone of his voice was clear, but the words stung nonetheless. Funny. They wouldn't have bothered her at all a week ago, she thought. Now it hurt that he would ever think of her that way. She hadn't been that awful—she'd only wanted to put order to the chaos and bring a little rationality to the haywire emotions after her mother and sister's awful accident.

"Hey." She turned at the sound of his voice to find him sitting upright beside her again. "Amelia, I know better now. I know you. I'm not judging you—then or now."

Pricks of miniscule teardrops stung her eyes, the result of extreme embarrassment—and profound relief. She had no idea what to make of the reaction. It was neither logical nor something she ever remembered experiencing.

"I know."

To her horror, the roughness of her emotions shone through her voice, and Gabriel peered at her, his face a study in surprise. "Are you crying? Amelia, I'm sorry—I was just giving you grief, I wasn't—"

"I'm not crying." Her insistence held no power even though it wasn't a lie. No water fell from her eyes; it just welled behind the lids. "I'm not upset. I'm . . . relieved. I . . . it was nice, what you . . . said." She clamped her mouth closed before something truly stupid emerged and looked down at the blanket, picking at a pill in the wool's plaid pile.

A touch beneath her chin drew her gaze back up. Gabriel's eyes were mere inches from hers, shining with that beautiful caramel brown that suddenly looked like it could liquefy into pure sweetness and sex. Every masculine pore of his skin caught her attention and made her fingers itch to stroke the texture of his cheek. The scent of wind-blown skin and chocolate tantalized her.

"Don't be anything but what and who you are, Amelia Crockett."

His kiss brushed her mouth with the weightlessness of a Monarch on a flower petal. Soft, ethereal, tender, it promised nothing but a taste of pleasure and asked for nothing in return. Yet, as subtle as it was, it drove a punch of desire deep into Mia's core and then set her stomach fluttering with anticipation.

He pulled back but his fingers remained on her chin. "I'm sorry. That was probably uncalled for."

When his fingers, too, began to slide from her skin, she reacted without thinking and grabbed his hand. "No. It's . . .

It was . . . Gah—" Frustrated by her constant, unfamiliar loss for words, she leaned forward rather than let mortification set in and pressed a kiss against his lips this time, foregoing light and airy for the chance to taste him fully. Beneath the pressure, his lips curved into a smile. She couldn't help it then, her mouth mimicked his and they clashed in a gentle tangle of lips, teeth, and soft, surprised chuckles.

"Crazy," he said in a whisper, as he encircled her shoulders and pulled her closer.

"Yeah," she agreed and opened her mouth to invite his tongue to meet hers.

First kisses in Mia's experience were usually fraught with uncertainty and awkwardness about what should come next, but not this one. Kissing Gabriel seemed as natural and pleasurable as walking along a stunning stream full of rapids and eddies and satisfying things to explore. She explored them all and let him taste and enjoy right back. When at last they let each other go, her head continued to spin with surprise, and every nerve ending sparkled with desire.

An Excerpt from

RESCUED BY THE RANGER

by Dixie Lee Brown

Army Ranger Garrett Harding is new in
town—but not necessarily welcome. The only
thing Rachel Maguire wants is to send this
muscled military man packing. But when the
stalker who destroyed her life ten years ago
reappears, Rachel hits the road hoping to lure
danger away from those she loves. Garrett
won't let this sexy spitfire face trouble alone.
He'll do anything to protect her. Even if it
means risking his life—and his heart.

Pressed tight to the wall, Garrett waited. As she burst from cover, looking over her right shoulder and away from him, he stepped toward her. Catching her around the middle, he swung her off her feet and up against his body, holding her tightly with both arms. "It's me, Rach. Take it easy. I just want to talk."

She stopped struggling, so he loosened his hold as he set her back on her feet. Mistake number one. She dug her fingernails into his forearm, scratching until she drew blood. As soon as he leaned over her shoulder to grab her hand, she whacked his jaw with the back of her head, hard enough to send him stumbling back a step. He shook his head to clear the stars in time to see her swing that black bag.

"Wait a minute, Rachel!" Garrett tried to duck, but her shorter height gave her the advantage. She caught him across the side of the head, and there was apparently something heavy and damn hard in her bag. He staggered, lost his balance, and went down.

She looked surprised for a second before determination steeled her expression. "I told you not to look for me. What didn't you understand about that?" Shifting her bag onto her shoulder, she turned, and started running down the alley.

"Well, shit." Garrett glanced at Cowboy and damned if it didn't look like he was laughing. "Okay, already. You were right. Saddle up, Cowboy."

The dog took off, his long strides closing the distance to Rachel's retreating back easily. Garrett stood, brushing the dirt off and taking a moment to stretch the ache from the wound in his back. Then he jogged after the girl and the dog. He'd seriously underestimated Rachel today. Cowboy had his instructions to stop her, but keeping her there would require a whole different set of commands—ones that Garrett would never utter where Rachel was concerned.

Ahead of him, the dog ran circles around her, making the circle smaller each time. When she finally stopped, keeping a wary eye on the animal, Cowboy dropped to a walk, his tail wagging as he angled toward her. Though she didn't move, her body, tense and ready, said she was on high alert. Garrett picked up his pace to reach them.

Rachel looked over her shoulder, obviously noted the diminishing distance between them, and grabbed for her satchel. The next thing he knew, the damn hard object she'd hit him with—a small revolver—was in her hand and she was pointing it at Cowboy.

"You need to stay where you are, Garrett, and call your dog or . . . I'll shoot him."

"Cowboy, chill." The dog dropped to the ground, watching Garrett carefully. "This is what it's come to then? You want to get away from me so bad you're willing to shoot my dog?"

She shook her head dejectedly. "That's not what I want, but I will if I have to."

"I don't believe you, Rach. That dog's just following orders. My orders. Shoot me if you want to hurt somebody." Garrett moved a few steps closer.

Rachel laughed scornfully. "Did you miss the part where I tried to leave without anybody getting hurt?"

"No. I get that you're worried about Peg, Jonathan, and the rest of the people at the lodge, but damn it, Rachel, they love you. They want to understand. They want to help if they can, because that's what people do when they love someone. They don't sneak off in the night, leaving their *family* to wonder what happened."

"I can't—" She lowered the weapon until her hand hung at her side. Her eyes closed for a second, then she sat abruptly amidst the grass that bordered the alley.

Garrett walked up to her and knelt down. Prying the gun from her fingers, he placed it back in her bag and zipped it up. "Yes, you can. I'll help you." He tilted her chin up so he could see the sheen of her expressive green eyes. "Give me a chance, Rachel. What have you got to lose?"

An Excerpt from

ONE SCANDALOUS KISS
An Accidental Heirs Novel

by Christy Carlyle

When a desperate Jessamin Wright bursts
into an aristocratic party and shocks the
entire ton, she believes it's the only way to
save her failing bookstore. The challenge
sounded easy when issued, but the one thing
she never expected was to enjoy the outrageous
embrace she shares with a serious viscount.

For the hundredth time, Jess called herself a fool for agreeing to Kitty Adderly's ridiculous plan for revenge against Viscount Grimsby. Kissing a viscount for one hundred pounds sounded questionable at the time Kitty had suggested it. Now Jess thought perhaps the jilted heiress had put something in her tea.

Initially she made her way into the crowded art gallery unnoticed, but then a woman dripping in diamonds and green silk had questioned her. When the lady's round husband stepped in, it all turned to chaos before she'd even done what she'd come to do. The deed itself shouldn't take long. A quick peck on the mouth—Kitty had insisted that she kiss the man on the lips—and it would all be over. She'd already handed the money over to Mr. Briggs at the bank. Turning back now simply wasn't an option.

She recognized Lord Grimsby from the gossip rag Kitty had shown her. The newspaper etching hadn't done him justice. In it, he'd been portrayed as dark and forbidding, his mouth a sharp slash, his black brows so large they overtook his eyes, and his long Roman nose dominating an altogether unappealing face. But in the flesh every part of his appearance harmonized into a striking whole. He was the sort of man she would have noticed in a crowd, even if she hadn't been seeking him, intent on causing him scandal and taking unimaginable liberties with his person.

He was there at the end of the gallery, as far from the entrance as he could possibly be. Jess continued through the gamut and a man snatched at her arm. Unthinking, she stepped on his foot, and he spluttered and cursed but released her.

Lord Grimsby saw her now. She noticed his dark head—and far too many others—turned her way. He was tall and broad shouldered, towering over the man and woman beside him. And he did look grim, as cold and disagreeable as Kitty had described.

Jessamin turned her eyes down, avoiding his gaze. Helpfully, the crowd parted before her, as if the respectable ladies and gentlemen were unwilling to remain near a woman behaving so unpredictably. Every time she raised her eyes, she glimpsed eyes gone wide, mouths agape, and women furiously fanning themselves.

Just a few more steps and Jess stood before him, only inches between them. She met his gaze and found him glaring down at her with shockingly clear blue eyes. Furrowed lines formed a vee between his brows as he frowned at her like a troublesome insect had just spoiled his meal.

She opened her mouth to speak, but what explanation could she offer?

Every thought scattered as she studied her objective—or more accurately, his lips. They were wide and well-shaped but firmly set. Not as firm as stone, as Kitty claimed, but unyielding. Unwelcoming. Not at all the sort of lips one dreamed of kissing. But Jess had given up on dreams. Her choices now were about money, the funds she needed to keep the bookshop afloat for as long as she could.

Taking a breath and praying for courage, Jess reached up and removed her spectacles, folded them carefully, and hooked them inside the high neckline of her gown.

His eyes followed the movement of her hands, and the lines between his brows deepened.

Behind her, a woman shouted, "How dare you!" A hand grasped her from behind, the force of the tug pulling Jessamin backward, nearly off her feet. Then a deep, angry male voice rang out and stopped all movement.

"Unhand the woman. Now, if you please." He'd spoken. The stone giant. Lord Grim. He glared past her, over her head. Whoever gripped her arm released their hold. Then Lord Grim's gaze drilled into hers, his eyes discerning, not cold and lifeless as she'd expected.

For several heartbeats he simply watched her, pinning her with his gaze, studying her. Jess reminded herself to breathe.

"Are we acquainted, madam?"

The rumble of his voice, even amid the din of chatter around them, echoed through her.

She moved closer, and his eyebrows shot up. Oh, she'd crossed the line now. Bursting uninvited into a room filled with the wealthy and titled was one thing. Ignoring a viscount's question could be forgiven. Pressing one's bosom into a strange man's chest was something else entirely.

A surge of surprise and gratitude gripped her when he didn't move away.

Assessing his height, Jess realized she'd have to lift onto her toes if the kiss was to be accomplished. She took a step toward him, stretched up tall, and swayed unsteadily. He reached an arm out, and she feared he'd push her away. Instead he gripped her arm just above her elbow and held her steady.

A woman said his name, a tone of chastisement lacing the word. "Lucius."

Then she did it. Placing one hand on his hard chest to balance herself, Jess eased up on the tips of her boots and touched her lips to his.

An Excerpt from

DIRTY TALK
A Mechanics of Love Novel
by *Megan Erickson*

Brent Payton has a reputation for wanting to have fun, all the time. It's well-earned after years of ribbing his brothers and flirting with every girl he meets, but he's more than just a good time, even though nobody takes the time to see it. When a new girl walks into his family's garage with big thoughtful eyes and legs for days, this mechanic wants something serious for the first time.

Ivy Dawn is done with men, all of them. She and her sister uprooted their lives for them too many times and she's not willing to do it again. Avoiding the opposite sex at all costs seems easy enough, until the sexy mechanic with the dirty mouth bursts into her life.

Brent was the middle brother, the joker, the comic relief. The irresponsible one.

Never mind that he'd been working at this shop since he was sixteen. Never mind that he could do every job, inside and out, and fast as fuck.

Never mind that he could be counted on, even though no one treated him like that.

A pain registered in his wrist and he glanced down at the veins and tendons straining against the skin in his arm where he had a death grip on a wrench.

He loosened his fist and dropped the tool on the bench.

This wallowing shit had to stop.

This was his life. He was happy (mostly) and free (no ball and chain, no way) and so what if everyone thought he was a joke? He was good at that role, so the type-casting fit.

"Why so glum, sugar plum?" Alex said from beside him as she peered up into his face.

He twisted his lips into a smirk and propped a hip on the counter, crossing his arms over his chest. "I knew you had a crush on me, sweet cheeks."

She narrowed her eyes, lips pursed to hide a smile. "Not even in your dreams."

He sighed dramatically. "You're just like all the ladies. Wanna piece of Brent. There's enough to go around, Alex, no need to butter me up with sweet nicknames—"

A throat cleared. And Brent looked over to see a woman standing beside them, one hand on her hip, the other dangling at her side holding a paper bag. Her dark eyebrows were raised, full red lips pursed.

And Brent blinked, hoping this wasn't a mirage.

Tory, Maryland, wasn't big, and he'd made it his mission to know every available female in the town limits, and about a ten mile radius outside of that.

This woman? He'd never seen her. He'd surely remembered if he had.

Gorgeous. Long hair so dark brown, it was almost black. Perfect face. It was September, and still warm, so she wore a tight striped sundress that ended mid-thigh. She was tiny, probably over a foot smaller than him. Fuck, the things that little body made him dream about. He wondered if she did yoga. Tiny and limber was his kryptonite.

Narrow waist, round hips, big tits.

No ring.

Bingo.

He smiled. Sure, she was probably a customer, but this wouldn't be the first time he'd managed to use the garage to his advantage. Usually he just had to toss around a tire or two, rev an engine, whatever, and they were more than eager to hand over a phone number and address. No one thought he was a consummate professional anyway, so why bother trying to be one?

He leaned his ass against the counter, crossing his arms over his chest. "Can I help you?"

She blinked, long lashes fluttering over her big blue eyes. "Can you help me?"

"Yeah, we're full service here." He resisted winking. That was kinda sleazy.

Her eyes widened for a fraction before they shifted to Alex at his side, then back to him. Her eyes darkened for a minute, her tongue peeked out between those red lips, then she straightened. "No, you can't help me."

He leaned forward. "Really? You sure?"

"Positive."

"Like, how positive?"

"I'm one hundred percent positive that I do not need help from you, Brent Payton."

That made him pause. She knew his name. He knew he'd never met her so that could only mean that she heard about him somehow and by the look on her face, it was nothing good.

Well shit.

He opened his mouth, not sure what to say, but hoping it came to him when Alex began cracking up next to him, slapping her thighs and snorting.

Brent glared at her. "And what's your problem?"

Alex stepped forward, threw her arm around the shoulder of the woman in front of them and smiled ear to ear. "Brent, meet my sister, Ivy. Ivy, thanks for making me proud."

They were both smiling now, that same full-lipped, white-teethed smile. He surveyed Alex's face, then Ivy's, and holy fuck, how did he not notice this right away? They almost looked like twins.

And the sisters were looking at him now, wearing matching smug grins and wasn't that a total cock-block. He pointed at Alex. "What did you tell her about me?"

"That the day I interviewed, you asked me to recreate a Whitesnake music video on the hood of a car."

He threw up his hands. "Can you let that go? You weren't even my first choice. I wanted Cal's girlfriend to do it."

"Because that's more appropriate," Alex said drily.

"Excuse me for trying to liven it up around here."

Ivy turned to her sister, so he got a better glimpse of those thighs he might sell his soul to touch. She held up the paper bag. "I brought lunch, hope that's okay."

"Of course it is," Alex said. "Thanks a lot, since someone stole my breakfast." She narrowed her eyes at Brent. Ivy turned to him slowly in disbelief, like she couldn't believe he was that evil.

Brent had made a lot of bad first impressions in his life. A dad of one of his high school girlfriends had seen Brent's bare ass while Brent was laying on top of his daughter before the dad ever saw Brent's face. That had not gone over well. And yet this one might be even worse.

Because he didn't care about what that girl's dad thought of him. Not really.

And he didn't want to care about what Ivy thought of him, but dammit, he did. It bothered the hell out of him that she'd written him off before even meeting him. Did Alex tell her any of his good qualities? Like . . . Brent wracked his brain for good qualities.

By the time he thought of one, the girls had already disappeared to the back room for lunch.